PUFFIN BOOKS

UK | USA | Canada | Ireland | Australia
India | New Zealand | South Africa

Puffin Books is part of the Penguin Random House group of companies
whose addresses can be found at global.penguinrandomhouse.com.

www.penguin.co.uk
www.puffin.co.uk
www.ladybird.co.uk

Originally published in the Portuguese language in Brazil by Editora Nemo, 2015
English-language edition first published in Great Britain by Puffin Books, 2016

001

Typeset in 12/19 pt Sabon
Printed in Great Britain by Clays Ltd, St Ives plc

A CIP catalogue record for this book is available from the British Library

ISBN: 978-0-141-37374-4

All correspondence to
Puffin Books
Penguin Random House Children's
80 Strand, London WC2R ORL

JIM ANOTSU

THE SWORD OF HEROBRINE

PUFFIN

CONTENTS

CHAPTER 1

ZEROS AND ONES

Fifteen-year-old Arthur didn't have much planned for that evening. Maybe he'd watch *Bleach* or read the latest issue of *Spider-Man*. After all, Miles Morales was always good company. Arthur definitely wasn't intending to play Minecraft or look after his younger sister – those were pretty much his least favourite things to do. But you don't always get what you wish for.

Everything seemed normal. Arthur's parents had gone to one of their boring events and his sister was sitting down at the living-room computer, playing that stupid game of blocks. Not that Arthur hated games or anything. He knew everything about *Assassin's Creed*, *Metal Gear Solid* and *Halo* – he just didn't understand how something with such basic graphics and squares could appeal to anyone.

'I'm hungry,' Mallu whined. 'Mum said you'd be cooking dinner tonight.'

Arthur looked away from the TV.

'You've got two hands,' he told her, in the snappy tone he always used with his sister. 'You can take a break from that game and cook dinner – now it's my turn to use the computer.'

Mallu had long curly hair and the same caramel-coloured skin as her brother. Arthur thought she had every flaw you could possibly have, the worst being her age: fourteen years of nuisance. Just as bad were her huge brown eyes and her blackmailing voice.

'If you don't cook dinner, I'll tell Mum and then you'll be punished for the rest of your life.'

'I hate you.'

'I don't care!'

Arthur threw the remote control on to the sofa and walked towards the kitchen. It was always the same. When his parents were away, they practically forced him to be his sister's slave. If she complained about anything, he was punished. '*Arthur didn't cook dinner. He hit me, he swore, he did this, he did that.*' It was a long list that could cover pages and pages, and almost all the things Mallu said weren't true. It wasn't that they hated each other. They might occasionally even manage to be polite and kind to one other – on special occasions and leap years, and as long as no one was looking. But as far as Arthur was concerned, there must have been a universal law that kept younger sisters from being cool.

And if there isn't one, Arthur thought, *someone should write it into the constitution of the universe.*

'*So* annoying!' he muttered.

He went to the kitchen drawer, looking for a knife. He only knew how to make scrambled eggs on toast, something his sister liked, as she could eat it without having to stop playing. Imagine what would happen if she couldn't play Minecraft, even for one day. Would she fall on the floor twitching? Or would she just stay in a corner without eating or uttering a word? *A question worth exploring*, Arthur thought to himself.

3

He pulled out the drawer and was stunned by what he found. Inside, among all the usual things you'd find in a kitchen drawer, there was a grey floppy disc labelled in red: MINECRAFT 001. There was no question as to whose it was. There was only one person in the house who left things all over the place – and played Minecraft.

Arthur grabbed the disc and headed back to the living room. This time Mallu wouldn't be able to deny it and blame it on him.

'Hey, loser,' he said sharply. 'Are you missing something?'

Mallu said nothing and kept breaking blocks in the game on the screen. She was playing in some sort of cave with tracks on its floor.

'I'm talking to you.'

'I'm busy, Arthur,' she said.

Arthur sighed. 'Of all places, you left your stupid game in one of the kitchen drawers.'

Mallu turned round to look at him for the first time, bewildered, as if what Arthur had said made no sense to her. 'I didn't leave anything in the kitchen,' she said.

'So what's this then?'

Mallu stared at the floppy disc Arthur was waving between his index finger and thumb. She had a frown on her face, and Arthur almost believed her expression of disbelief.

Almost.

'Anything to say?'

She stood up and grabbed the plastic square from his hand the way a palaeontologist might grab their latest fossil. Arthur was sure she was just trying to find an excuse to go back to playing Minecraft.

In the end, she put the disc on the computer desk and said, 'The only thing I have to say is that you're totally clueless.' She grinned as though this was hilarious. 'If you were smart, you would have noticed it was Daddy's handwriting, not mine. Another detail you missed: I play Minecraft with my friends *online*. And thirdly . . . Man, floppy discs are so old-fashioned. No one uses them any more.'

Arthur said nothing, wondering how he could have missed those details. All he had wanted was to catch his sister red-handed. He should have realized that when Minecraft came out, floppy discs were already a thing of the past. But he couldn't figure out what his dad had to do with Minecraft. His doubtful expression must have given him away, because his sister said, 'Unless Dad wanted to keep some kind of secret from us, then I don't think he would mind if we had a look.' She smirked. 'Especially as he wouldn't know we'd done it.'

Arthur cracked his knuckles as he always did when he was nervous. One of their family rules was never to touch anything that belonged to someone else without their permission.

Arthur tried to be sensible. 'I think we'd better put it back in the drawer and forget about it,' he said.

'You can forget about it if you want,' Mallu said. 'But I'm way too curious to ignore it. And if Dad finds out . . . Well, if he does, I'll just blame it on you.'

'You are so shameless.'

'Yep,' she said. 'Honestly. Why are boys such cowards?'

She'd made the threat like it was a joke, but Arthur knew that if something did go wrong, she really would blame it on him.

Well, if he was going to be framed, he had better find out what he was being blamed for.

He pushed his sister aside and sat next to her as the floppy disc was swallowed by the CPU.

CHAPTER 2

THE MESSAGE

OIOIOIIOOIIOIIIIOIIOOOIIIIIOIOIOOOIOOOOO
OIIOIOIOIIIOOOOIOOIOOOOOOIIIOIIOOIIOIOOI
OIIIO IOIOOIOOOOOOIIOIIIIOOIOOOOOOIOOIOO
OOIIOOIOIOIOIIOOIOOIIOIIIIOIIOOOIOOIIIOOI
OOIIOIOOIOI IOIIIOOIIOOIOIOOIIIIIIIOOIOOO
OOOIOOOIOIOIIOIIOIOOIOOOOOOIIIOOIIOIIIOI
OIOIIOOOOIOOIOOOO OOIIOOOIIOIIOOOOIOIIIO
OIIOIIOOOOIOOIOOOOOOIIOIIIOOIIOIIIIOOIOO
OOOOIOOIIIOOIIOOIOIOIII OIOOOIIOIOOOOIIO
OIOIOIIIOOIOOOIOIIOOOOIOOOOOOIIOIIIIOOIO
OOOOOIIOIIOIOIOIIOIIIIOIIIOOIOO IIIOIOOOII
OIIIIOOIOOO●OOIOOIOOOOIIOOIOIOIOIIOOIOOII
OIIIIOIIOOOIOOIIIOOIOOIIOIOIOOIOIIOII IOOI

THE MESSAGE

IOOIOIOOIOOOOOOIIOOOOIOIIOOIIIOIIIOIOIOI

IOOOOIOIIIOOIOOIIOOIOOOIIOOOOIOOIOOOOOOO

II   IOOIIOIIOIIIIOIIOIIIOOIIOIOOOOIIOOOOI

OIIOIIIOOIIOOIOOOIIOIIIIOOIOIOIIIO

CHAPTER 3

DIGITAL CONVERSATIONS

Blue screen. *Zero. One. Zero. One.* White numbers appeared . . . and nothing more. Arthur and Mallu looked at each other. Maybe they'd just wrecked the computer with a super-virus.

A few more creaks, as if the computer's CPU was trying to process more than it could cope with. Some more clicking noises.

'Turn it off,' shouted Arthur. 'Turn it off *now*!'

More numbers and noises.

'I'm trying, I'm trying!' said Mallu, pressing hard on the power button. But it didn't work – the numbers kept flashing on the screen, a waterfall of incomprehensible symbols.

Mallu was about to pull the plug out when

everything changed in an instant. And an instant can last forever when things are going wrong.

The screen went completely green. No numbers or letters. Just green.

'Do you think it's over?' asked Mallu.

'I have no idea.'

The screen gleamed brighter. It was so dazzling that it lit the whole living room with a green glow, blinding them both. Arthur covered his eyes with his hand and fell to the floor, groping for the plug and pulling it out of the socket.

'Arthur, help me, please!' screamed Mallu. 'It's pulling me . . . it's pulling me in!'

Arthur reached out for his sister but she had vanished.

Suddenly, as if nothing had happened, the green glow disappeared. The room was back to normal. Just an ordinary quiet night.

'Mallu?' Arthur called. 'Are you all right?'

His heart was beating fast, pounding in his chest. His mouth was dry, his fingertips were cold and his stomach twisted with fear. It took him a while to get used to the light. Every corner of the flat slowly came back into focus – the sofa's worn-out legs, the colourful cushions, the table, the computer . . . and his sister's disappearance.

He looked around frantically, but there was no trace of Maria Luísa Carvalho. And with every second that passed, Arthur felt more and more bewildered.

The computer screen was still green and filled with numbers, even though the disconnected plug lay by his feet.

Numbers.

Zeros and ones.

Arthur stepped forward and looked at the symbols on the screen. He had read about that kind of numerical sequence in a gaming magazine. It was something from 1960s computing: binary code. A sequence of the numbers one and zero which could conceal any message. He stared at the lines of numbers in front of him.

Then Arthur searched through the whole flat. He checked in every room – the bathroom, the bedroom wardrobes, the basement – but there was no sign of Mallu anywhere.

Then and there, his hope that Mallu might have been playing a trick on him was gone. In that moment, he thought about something Sherlock Holmes had once said: 'Once you eliminate the impossible, whatever remains, no matter how improbable, must be the truth.' Well, he'd already ruled out everything that was possible and everything that was unlikely, so perhaps the time had come to brace himself for the impossible – especially as this involved a computer that had been turned off . . . and yet was still on.

He stood in front of the computer and looked at the numbers. 'Why don't you work in a way I understand?' he muttered in exasperation.

As if in reply, there was a *blip*. The computer's CPU creaked and whirred, processing something. It gave Arthur the creeps. The numbers turned into letters which made up just one question: ENTER THE OVERWORLD?

'What?' Arthur said with a start.

The question remained on the screen, as if waiting for the boy to answer, although he didn't have a clue how he was supposed to do that.

What on earth is the Overworld? Some sort of program? he wondered. *Or some part of a computer that I don't know about?*

Mallu knew all about electronics and software and things, but Arthur didn't have the slightest idea about that stuff. He *did* know how to freestyle rap and he could recite the names of 150 Pokémon by heart, but that wasn't much use right now.

With no other options left, he sat down in front of the monitor and decided to try one last thing.

'I want my sister back,' he said. 'I know you can understand me. That's why that message appeared, right? So where is my sister?'

The CPU creaked and replaced the previous question with a single word written in giant letters: OVERWORLD.

That wasn't much help, as Arthur didn't know what that word meant, and he was already at the limit of his computer knowledge. He slapped the monitor.

'You stupid thing, bring my sister back!' he shouted. 'Even if that means me having to pull her out of you!'

Then it was the machine's turn to answer. There was a *blip*, and two words flashed on the screen.

COMMAND ACCEPTED.

There was nothing Arthur could do. The screen glowed green once more and suddenly he felt very strange. It was as if each part of his body was being taken apart, the little pieces falling away like discarded breadcrumbs.

Arthur had no idea that his body had left the real world. He was being taken to a faraway place, a place more frightening and incredible than anywhere else that had ever existed.

The Overworld's door lay wide open.

PART ONE: GEOGRAPHY

By Punk-Princess166

Think of the weirdest place you can imagine – it will never be as odd as the Overworld, a world that isn't ruled by our laws of physics. And I say 'a world' because there are other worlds, such as the Nether and the End – but it's not the time to delve into them yet.

So let's talk about the Overworld, and about how the rule book's been thrown out of the window here. You can take away part of the trunk of a tree and the rest of the tree will still remain standing, just floating as if nothing has happened. But not everything is affected by gravity in the same way.

You want an example?

Floating trees won't fall to earth, but if you're mining gravel or sand, those blocks *will* fall, and they could even bury and kill you. Everything is a little strange in the Overworld, like a dream you can't apply too much logic to – if you try, it'll drive you crazy.

Geographically, the Overworld is made up of biomes. You can find a forest biome that stretches over a thousand kilometres right next to an ice biome, just a step away from one another. The same applies to other biomes, such as deserts and oceans. It's dead easy to get lost, so you should always carry a map and compass, especially when night falls.

Day and night are interesting in the Overworld. Day is the time when people work, do what needs doing and walk around freely, but night is a whole other story. Night is the time for monsters and horrible creatures, the time when your life chances are cut down dramatically, so you really need to ask yourself if it's worth venturing out of your home.

P.S. Monsters come out of nowhere. All they need is night-time or a dark place. Watch out for the creepers!

CHAPTER 4

A FOREST OF NIGHT AND PIXELS

Arthur's senses returned slowly, as if they had gone off on a journey to the other side of the world before strolling back on foot. His sense of smell recovered first, bringing with it the scent of an old computer, like one you might find in a second-hand furniture shop. A cold wind brushed his skin. His head throbbed. It took a while for him to remember what had happened – and to realize that it hadn't been a dream.

Arthur put his hands on the ground to help himself up, making an effort to open his eyes as the sunlight glared down at him. *Calm down*, he told himself. *You just need to be calm*. He didn't really think telling himself that would help, but he tried to believe that it would, as if it was advice from some self-help book. He looked around and soon regretted having believed that thinking would solve anything.

'What the . . .'

Everything was different. Every blade of grass, every leaf, every stone and every tree – they all seemed to be square, like pixels and Lego blocks. There were square trees, square stones and even little square animals. No amount of thinking could change what he was seeing; nothing made sense.

Every thought started and ended with the same conclusion.

I'm in a video game.

With no other option left, Arthur started walking. *There must be a way to find my sister and bring her back home*, he thought. Wondering if he had gone mad, Arthur took his first steps in this other world. Everything felt different, as if his hands were passing over polystyrene foam. He felt the texture of pixels on his skin too, and the sensation was so strange he couldn't even describe it.

He walked aimlessly – walking was much better than standing still. He couldn't believe he was inside

Minecraft, although everything pointed to the fact he was. He wished Mallu was with him – she knew everything about blocks and pixels. He knew nothing about this place and that could very well lead him to his death.

Arthur was deep in thought when he heard a voice calling from far away.

'Helloooooo!' someone yelled. 'Is anybody out there?'

Arthur froze. It was his sister's voice! He looked around; the sound seemed to be coming from somewhere on his left. His heart was beating fast, pounding in his chest. He ran as fast as he could without looking back. He needed to keep going – Mallu was near, somewhere among all these pixels. He could make out something in the distance, near a ravine full of undergrowth.

'Hey, I'm here!' he shouted. He couldn't let her get any further away. 'Please wait for me!'

She turned quickly. Silence fell as they stared at each other, their eyes roving up and down, checking every detail, every patch of skin, every movement, the way a tiger does to discern friend from foe.

'What are you doing here?' Mallu blurted out. Arthur could see that his sister was as shocked as he was. 'You idiot, you could have died! What if a monster had caught you?'

Arthur was relieved to see her, despite the lack of a warm welcome. Mallu looked tired – her face was covered in cuts and scratches, her clothes dirty, her hair dishevelled, like she'd just been pulled out of a ditch.

'What happened to your face?' he asked. 'I was with you just five minutes ago!'

Mallu shook her head. 'No, Arthur, you definitely weren't,' she said. 'I've been here for over three hours.'

That last comment made Arthur's eyes pop out of his head. He began to wonder whether his sister had gone mad.

'That's hard to believe,' he replied. 'I saw you at home just a few minutes ago.'

'Hard to believe? I don't think you've realized where we are right now.' Mallu grinned for the first time since they had found each other. 'It may have been minutes out there, but it's been hours in here.'

'What is this place?' Arthur looked around him, taking in the trees and the forest, which ran all the way down the ravine. Everything was bright and colourful, but it was also quiet and frightening. Just silence and trees.

'Haven't you realized yet? We're in the Minecraft Overworld, home to all kinds of creepers, endermen, zombies and skeletons. Be my guest and walk into the world of blocks.'

Arthur gazed at the world that was unfolding before his eyes, seriously regretting not having played Minecraft before. Then at least he would know what the Overworld was, and what endermen and creepers were. Luckily he already knew what zombies and skeletons were.

The only good thing was that Mallu knew this place better than anyone. So if he was going to make it home in one piece, he was going to have to rely on her.

'Well, somehow we have to get back home,' he said sheepishly. 'Mallu, do you know how to get back?'

'First off,' she said, scratching her chin, 'if we're in

the game world, we'd better stick to our usernames. Can you please call me Punk-Princess166?'

Arthur smiled tightly, trying to be patient. 'Don't you think that's a bit difficult to say?'

'No,' Mallu replied. 'I think it's as good a name as any other. So what's your username?'

'Stop getting excited about this place, and start trying to get us out of here! I just want to get back home.'

'A boy without a name? Well, I'm going to call you Arthur, or Noobie Saibot, until you find your real name.'

'I'm starting to regret coming after you.'

'You love me really, Noobie.'

Arthur started to say something but was cut off when he heard a noise like the hiss of a cobra, and smelled something like a whiff of a burning fuse – the tang of gunpowder and fire.

He was about to spin round when Punk-Princess166 gave him such a huge shove that the world around him spun round instead. Again and again he spun as his body rolled down the ravine, battered by plants and stones. Arthur wished he could say he faced the ordeal with great courage but in fact he screamed his head off the whole way.

'Will you stop screaming!' Punk-Princess166 shouted. 'You'll lure them closer! Stop screaming!'

Arthur was too busy crying out for help on his 'trip'. His roll down the ravine only lasted for a few seconds but it seemed endless. All he could manage were a few out-of-tune musical notes so loud that they would have made an opera singer jealous. The end was the most painful part – he finally crashed into a huge tree. He was winded and in pain, but happy to find that he hadn't fainted. While he was mustering the courage to get up and swear at his sister, everything around him suddenly flew into the air.

In an instant . . .

There was such a huge, loud, bright explosion that it made the ground shake and threw the earth at the top of the hill in all directions. Pixelated blocks scattered in millions of pieces, big and small, some fading like fireworks dying out in the sky. The blinding white glare dazzled him; he had tears in his eyes, his ears were buzzing, and every bit of his body was in agony. The only word he could let out then was a very bad one. Once again he boiled with hatred for the place in which he'd found himself. There was only one thought in his mind.

Damn Minecraft!

CHAPTER 5

LIFE AFTER THE CREEPER

'Mallu?' Arthur called out faintly. 'Are you OK?'

A loud groan answered his question. *Well at least we're both still alive*, he thought. He mustered all his courage, leaned to one side and rose to his feet. His brain was crammed full – he was still trying to work out how it had all happened.

He went straight to help his sister up amid the smoke. She had been hit as badly as he had – her face was covered in scratches. She had small cuts on her hands and was splattered in muck from head to toe. This kingdom she thought she was 'princess' of . . . it looked more like a pile of ash than a throne.

'Well, brother, may I have the pleasure of introducing you to your very first creeper,' she said.

'At least it isn't nightfall yet –'

Her explanation made no sense at all, so Arthur interrupted her with a question before she could even finish talking.

'What's a creeper?'

'Oh yeah,' she answered, 'I'd forgotten that you're a total newbie, the worst kind of noob. Creepers are the stupidest things in the Minecraft world – they're green monsters which blow up and destroy everything around them,' she explained. 'Monsters usually come out after nightfall, but they can also turn up in places like forests where there's some shadow.' She shrugged her shoulders like that was no big deal. 'Let's keep walking. You won't like it here after nightfall.'

Noobie Saibot and Punk-Princess166 started to walk aimlessly – they were lost anyway, so the path they took wouldn't make much difference. Arthur hobbled along, hungry and thirsty, and without the slightest idea about how much time had passed since he had landed there. It was as if his perception of time had changed, turning an hour into a minute, and stretching that minute out into a huge labyrinth.

Even though he was exhausted, there was one thing on his mind that he couldn't shake – something his sister had mentioned earlier.

'Mallu, you said monsters usually come out after nightfall. So does that mean there are lots of monsters here?'

'The name is Punk-Princess166,' she said, without looking away from the path. 'The Overworld is filled with monsters, so yeah, there's a lot of them. They roam about through the night trying to kill players, and so we make houses, tunnels and weapons to survive in the game. It's a wild world, my friend.'

How can we escape from here? How are we going to face all the dangers that seem to be lurking around in the Overworld? Arthur asked himself.

'Hey, Noobie,' Mallu called. 'There's something you need to see.'

Arthur approached the place she was pointing at: a tall tree with a ladder leaning against its trunk. Arthur suddenly realized then that there could be someone else here – perhaps a Minecraft player or even an adult who could help them escape. The glimmer of hope that just a second earlier had seemed so distant came back, although Arthur had to acknowledge that it was a pretty feeble hope, as all hopes seemed to be in Minecraft. He might as well face it – what was the use of a ladder leaning against a tree trunk when there were monsters that blew up all around you?

'Do you want to climb up?' Mallu asked, placing her right foot on the ladder. 'Maybe we can look out from the top and see if there are any villages nearby that we might be able to reach.'

'Good idea,' Arthur said. 'Surely climbing up a tree can't be worse than nearly getting blown up by a monster.'

'That's a good way to look at it.'

Punk-Princess166 started climbing up the ladder. She seemed fearless, and she didn't even look down as she climbed. Arthur hadn't realized Mallu *could* climb trees. He had to stop for a second to remind himself that she was the girl he used to argue with every day. He grabbed the wooden ladder tightly and began climbing, feeling that light electric shock which sprang from everything in this world.

Going up the first few rungs was as easy as playing in his little tree house at home, but things started changing after he'd climbed up about four metres. His hands ached and his own body weight felt unbearable. Arthur didn't like heights, whether it was standing near the window at the top of a skyscraper or travelling by plane. The few times he managed to glance down from the ladder, he felt a massive wave of ice fill his stomach, and he was pleased that it didn't spread any further and reach his pants.

While he was dealing with his own issues, Punk-Princess166 had managed to reach the top of the tree. Eventually Arthur did too, and he was relieved to find that the branches were thick and strong.

'This is pretty amazing, isn't it?' Mallu asked, looking out from the treetop. 'Being here may not be good news for us, but I could stand up here looking around for hours.'

Arthur followed the direction of her gaze. The sky was a smooth blue veil; it was about to get dark, and the setting sun was surrounded by twilight's orange shadow. The sun, like everything else that made up the Minecraft world, was a square; it shone in the digital heavens, as yellow as a piece of gold, giving off a different sort of warmth from the sun in Arthur's real world. Hotter, yet pleasantly so – programmed to be perfect.

But, despite all of that, Arthur couldn't forget what Mallu had said earlier: monsters came out after nightfall. That was the time of zombies and creepers, creatures capable of blowing up, and some of those monsters could kill them in just a second. That's right – *kill them*. Arthur already knew that he could get hurt in this world – the cuts on his face and the pain all over his body testified to that. And even if this was just a game, he didn't fancy trying his luck and dying.

'Do you think we stand any chance of making it back home?' Arthur asked, his eyes still fixed on the slow descent of the square sun.

'I think *you'll* get back home,' Mallu said. 'It won't be that hard.'

'Don't you want to go home?'

'I haven't made up my mind yet.' Mallu sighed and changed the subject before Arthur had the chance to push the question.

'Look ahead, over there,' she said, pointing. 'There's a plain in that direction, which is always a good sign. All villages in Minecraft are found on the plains – the game's algorithm prevents you from creating them in forests. So that's where we should head for – that'll be our only chance of finding someone who can help us. Maybe another player.'

'Well, at least we know where to go now,' Arthur said. 'I hope we'll be able to get some food in that village. I'm starving.'

'I hope they have cake,' Mallu said cheerfully.

Arthur nodded. Yet again he wished he'd played Minecraft before, although he couldn't exactly have foreseen being sucked into it the way he had. He was grateful to have Punk-Princess166 by his side as he began climbing down the ladder. One step at a time, then faster, holding on so hard that his fingers turned white . . . Then all in a rush after realizing that most of the sky had already turned into a huge black shadow, driving the sun down over the horizon.

'Wandering around here at night is a sure-fire way to get killed,' Mallu told him. 'There isn't a tree here tall enough to keep skeletons from firing arrows at us, so we'll have to run as fast as we can until we reach the plain, where we can find shelter.'

'That doesn't sound like the best plan ever,' Arthur observed.

'That's all we can do. Either we die trapped up here, or we die being chased down there. But yeah. Neither is a great option.'

When they reached the ground, night had fallen across the Overworld, and they were still surrounded by the forest of pixels.

And, deep in the shadows of all those square trees, the two siblings were not alone.

They could hear noises that hinted at unpleasant company: groans, the sounds of things crashing and fighting for their lives, something dragging through dry leaves, screams and squeals, distorted sounds like an out-of-tune guitar. But nothing frightened Noobie Saibot and Punk-Princess166 more than the hundreds of bright red eyes that suddenly glowed all around them. Hundreds upon hundreds of eyes, staring at the two wanderers in the forest.

CHAPTER 6

RUN, USER, RUN

Any human being could in theory have enough energy to run for three days straight, doing an average of twenty-four kilometres an hour. But this would only be possible if the person was running on an open and unobstructed track, unlike Arthur and Punk-Princess166, who were running through a forest . . . at night. And they could hear enemies chasing after them. Given the circumstances, they would be lucky to keep this up for more than ten minutes without running out of energy. Under the light of the square moon, the two of them sprinted through the woods as fast as they could.

'Just keep running,' Punk-Princess166 shouted.

'And if you come across an enderman, don't try to fight it!'

'I don't even know what an enderman looks like!' Arthur yelled back.

'Lucky you,' Punk-Princess166 muttered.

They ran on through the forest; branches whipped Arthur's face and Punk-Princess166 stumbled, nearly falling. Arthur's legs ached. He felt like he was about to pass out, but panic kept him going. His fear spiked as the moonlight briefly revealed silhouettes of the creatures chasing after them: hordes of huge, long-legged red-eyed spiders, black legs clacking as they scuttled across the forest floor. Arthur couldn't imagine anything scarier.

'They're getting closer!' he said. A thread of spider web landed on his head. 'They're getting closer *very quickly*!'

Punk-Princess166 reached out and held her brother's hand tightly. Her fingers were hot and clammy; she squeezed his hand hard.

'Trust me, Noobie . . . I've noticed!' she said.

They'd been naive to think they'd be able to get away from the forest just by running through the trees until they reached the plain. But, suddenly, amid all the chaos and their growing panic, something astonishing happened. From out of nowhere a bright glow lit the whole forest for a second. As one, the spiders recoiled from the light.

'Come with me!' shouted Punk-Princess166. 'I think there might be a mine nearby!'

Arthur turned and saw a strange figure – not that 'strange' narrowed things down that much round here. The figure looked vaguely human, but he was made up of blocks, just like everything else in the Overworld. He wore silver armour and carried a sword that blazed with fire every time he slew an enemy. Arthur didn't have time to take in much more than that, but any help was better than none, so he and his sister ran after the man in silver armour.

They followed him along a path. The spiders were still close, but hope was in sight now: Arthur and Punk-Princess166 were getting closer to a small stone building set in a clearing in the forest. The clearing hadn't been visible earlier – Arthur wondered whether their companion had created it for them. The stone building in its centre had a door and a window; torches shone from either side of its entrance and from its roof.

'Get in at once,' said the warrior, 'and hold tight for a second.'

They didn't waste time responding; they rushed into the house, slamming the door behind them so hard that the walls shivered and fragments fell from the ceiling. The room within was sparsely furnished: just a bed, a table, some treasure chests scattered around and a wooden block with symbols written on it. Arthur couldn't read the symbols or work out what the block was used for. On their left when they entered was a hole in the floor, through which they could see the top of a ladder like the one they had found leaning against the tree in the forest. Arthur realized both ladders must belong to whoever lived in this strange place in the middle of the forest.

They could still hear the sounds of the fight on the other side of the door as the warrior's sword clashed against spiders' bodies and tree trunks.

'Who *is* that creature?' Arthur asked. He thought about saying 'what' instead of 'who', but didn't want to seem rude, or ungrateful for the warrior's help. 'Is he a monster too?'

Punk-Princess166 ignored him, taking in all the things scattered around the room: the bed, the chests, and the huge block with symbols on it. Later, she would tell him it was a crafting table, the Minecraft space designed to create objects. But for now she just stood and stared in silence. When she finally seemed to remember Arthur was even there, she answered him in a strangely cheerful voice.

'It was a human mob,' she said. 'Anything that moves around in Minecraft is a mob, even that creeper or those spiders that attacked us. But human mobs are more like us – they build houses, villages, equipment and weapons. And that's why we're trying to reach the plain – to find any mob that might be able to help us.'

'I thought we were looking for people.'

'As far as I know, we're the only real people here. I don't have a clue why we *are* here, Noobie, but we are officially the most unusual thing in this world right now.'

Arthur stared at her, bewildered, but just as he

opened his mouth to start asking questions he was cut off by the arrival of the silver-armoured warrior. The warrior's helmet was cracked, and his sword was stained with the enemy spiders' blood, but he was grinning as if he hadn't had that much fun for a long time.

'Welcome, Users,' he said, hugging them. Arthur felt self-conscious – he knew he was sweaty and smelly. 'You have no idea how happy I am that you're here. Grab a chair and make yourselves at home!'

Arthur and his sister looked at each other in surprise. They hadn't expected such a friendly welcome, especially after all the dangers they'd encountered in the Overworld so far. Arthur was glad to find at least one friendly creature there, although he supposed that just because the warrior was friendly it didn't necessarily mean he wouldn't kill them. Still, he was the closest thing to an ally they'd found so far. A part of Arthur was terrified of him, but the warrior *had* saved them from the spiders, so after hesitating for a few seconds Arthur grabbed a chair and sat down. Punk-Princess166 did the same, and the two of them faced the strange, square man with the silver armour.

'Thank you very much for helping us,' Arthur said. 'If you hadn't turned up, those spiders would have finished us off.'

The warrior nodded his head. 'You don't need to thank me,' he said. 'It's my duty to help Users in any way I possibly can. My name is Steve. I was once an adventurer like you are now, until I was shot in the knee by an arrow.'

'Sorry to hear that, man,' said Punk-Princess166.

Arthur folded his arms and made up his mind to ask something that had been bothering him ever since they started talking to Steve. A single word that Steve had said had caught Arthur's attention. Maybe it was the key to getting them home.

'Steve, you called us Users,' he began. 'What does that mean? Have you already seen other humans around here?'

The mob walked to the window, turning his back on Arthur and Punk-Princess166 as he gazed out at the monster-filled night, where spiders and creepers were in pursuit of their prey. Arthur began to get the impression that Steve was never going to answer him, when suddenly he took a deep breath and replied.

'Just one.' Steve paused. 'He arrived here many cycles ago. He looked like you, made up of that odd material called flesh. He dug his first mine not far from here, then built houses and reared animals. He was a peace-loving person, a friend of the mobs,' Steve continued in a deep voice. 'But looking after his own place and living with us wasn't enough for him. He became obsessed with redstone, using it to build giant machines that would destroy forests and kill any mob in their way. He called himself the Red King, and found a way to keep all the bad mobs under his control. Every creature that attacked us out there was working for him.'

'If you want to see something turn ugly, just put a human in it and wait,' said Punk-Princess166.

There was a silence. Arthur didn't like what he'd just heard at all. He was appalled to think another human being was behaving that way – not a fictional character or a computer program gone wrong, but a *person* who had chosen to hurt others deliberately.

A nasty kid who seemed to have a lot more power than he should . . . and a human, who might know how Arthur and his sister had been plucked from the safety of their home.

Arthur sighed. This so-called Red King was the only clue they had to help them find a way back from this place. They had to try and find him, even though that would mean taking a huge risk. They *had* to find a way to get back home.

'So how can we find him, Steve?' Arthur asked.

'Maybe there is something else you should know,' Steve said, with a grim laugh, laying his sword down on the ground beside him. 'You'd better brace yourselves. It's going to be a long night. I have a lot of things to tell you.'

STEVE'S STORY

A long time ago, the Overworld was different. There was a time before Users and mobs, when there were only zeros and ones drifting around the web. Then one day – or rather, one moment, as there was neither day nor night then – the Overworld came into being and began to open out in all directions. It continues to grow _ even today, spreading out into infinity, never stopping. And, while our Overworld was being created, another dimension was also in the making: the Nether. This was the Overworld's grim twin, a place filled with fire and fear, where endermen and other wicked enemies were spawned.

Deep in this place of lava and dread, a creature

was born – a wicked being whose very existence put the Overworld at risk. A creature bent on spreading fear and suffering. Many have forgotten his name, but I have not. His name was Herobrine. He set up armies that destroyed everything in his path. He was more powerful than any mob; everywhere he went, he consumed everything before him.

It was during that time of darkness that the Users came. Two human children, like you, made up of flesh rather than pixels. The Users joined the mobs who were not under the grip of Herobrine, and together they fought for many years.

The Users made the Diamond Sword, the only thing that could banish Herobrine to a far-off place outside the Overworld. The two Users walked up to Blacksmith's Mountain 1234 and there they fought against Herobrine. It was a long battle, but at its end the enemy was defeated and banished to an abyss in the Nether.

The world gradually recovered and returned to normality. But the First Users knew that our world was destined to face terrible enemies for all time. So they hid the Diamond Sword – the only thing that could defeat any enemy – in the Overworld. At that time the prophecy was written: when the Overworld is in danger, new Users shall come to its rescue.

And here you are . . . just when a new enemy has arisen. A creature that threatens to end our peace forever. Your mission is clear: to save the Overworld with the Diamond Sword.

It won't be easy. The Red King is not a program or a digital being like me. He is a User, so he too knows the legend of the Diamond Sword, and he too is searching for it. If he ever finds it, he will be invincible.

Children, if you want to get back home, you must first defeat the Red King and fulfil the prophecy. Find the sword that banished Herobrine. Only then will you be able to return to the safety of your home.

CONCEPTS OF THE OVERWORLD

PART TWO: Creepers

By Punk-Princess166

Creepers blow up. That's the main thing you need to know about these monsters. They are the creatures every Overworld adventurer dreads coming across, simply because they are a *total* pain in the neck.

Unlike the other monsters in the Overworld, they don't burn and disappear in daylight, so they can chase after you for much longer. And, believe me, if you're spotted by one of them, they will chase after you for days. Hiding inside your house won't get rid of them, because they will lie in wait by your door until you come out. And then, when you do . . . *BANG!*

And what does a creeper look like, you ask?

Their appearance is always the same: they're green and four-legged with a square head and black eyes. Spotting a creeper is dead easy, but once you've spotted them, it may already be too late. They blow themselves up just for the sake of killing you.

The good news is that destroying them isn't that hard, as long as you wear a suit of armour and carry a sword. Remember: if you hear a sound like a fuse burning down . . .

RUN!

CHAPTER 7

STEVE'S VILLAGE

Minecraft sunlight struck Arthur's face and woke him up with that mild, electrical heat he'd noticed the day before. His first thought was that he must have been dreaming, but then he realized it was true: he really was lost in an unknown land, apparently destined to fight against a boy who thought he was a king. Well, that was pretty much what Steve had told them.

Thinking about Steve brought back everything else the warrior had said last night. Even if only half of it was true, the challenge they faced was enormous. Where would they find the Diamond Sword?

'Damn it!' Arthur muttered.

He sat up and looked around. Steve was sleeping on a bed by the window; Punk-Princess166 lay on a mattress on the floor, drooling and snoring, with one of her legs sticking out from beneath her blanket. Arthur recalled how, just before they went to bed, Steve had built the mattress – Punk-Princess166 had said this was called 'crafting' in Minecraft. This was the first evidence Arthur had seen that the laws of physics from the real world didn't exist in the Overworld: Steve had placed a few objects such as wooden pieces on the block covered in symbols, and, in a split second, two red mattresses had appeared in the living room. 'It's a bit like magic,' his sister had explained. 'And this is a crafting table, so if you place the right materials on it in the right arrangement, you can create anything you want.'

But he couldn't spend any longer thinking about physics now. There was no time to waste – they needed to find a village. Arthur pulled on his trainers and walked over to nudge both Steve and Punk-Princess166, but it took a while for them to wake up. Arthur could never understand people who wanted to sleep through the whole day. As far as Arthur was concerned, sleeping was boring and overrated.

'Just five more minutes, please, Noobie,' pleaded Punk-Princess166. 'Just five minutes, pleeeeeeease.'

'Not even *one* minute!' replied Arthur. 'We have to find a way to get back home.'

Waking Steve was even harder. The warrior was so fast asleep that they had to pour a glass of water over his head. But as soon as they did that, Steve woke up screaming and clenching his fists as if he was holding a sword.

'Damn creepers!' he shouted.

Arthur and Punk-Princess166 retreated and waited until Steve was fully awake, which took about a minute more. Then they had milk and fruit for breakfast. Everything had a weird sour taste, like plastic. They packed all the things they would need and Steve gave them both a chequered wooden sword, each of which seemed lighter than a pencil.

The first step in their plan was simple: to walk to the closest village and seek help.

'Do you think the Diamond Sword from the

legend Steve told us is actually real?' asked Punk-Princess166. 'There are definitely diamond swords in the game of Minecraft, but here things seem to be a bit different.'

'What do you mean, a bit different?'

'In Minecraft, diamond swords are unusual, but you can find them,' Arthur's sister said. 'Doesn't sound like that's true here. Plus we haven't seen many animals yet, but in the game, forests are full of cows.'

'What, there are cows in the middle of the forest?'

Punk-Princess166 shrugged her shoulders. 'No one ever said Minecraft was anything like the real world, Noobie.'

They walked on for a while. Steve got rid of some obstacles with his sword and they followed behind him.

'The road used to be well kept,' he said, 'but because of attacks by monsters loyal to the Red King, maintenance work has been impossible, so everything is dumped all over the place now.'

'Well, we're going to sort that out,' said Punk-Princess166. 'We just need to find the shining sword.'

'The Diamond Sword,' corrected Steve.

'If it's made of diamond, that means it shines, so it is a shining sword,' Punk-Princess166 retorted.

'Ah,' the warrior said. 'I guess that's true!'

Arthur kept quiet and carried on walking. He thought about home and all the things he would have liked to be doing; even washing the dishes would have been better than wandering around here searching for a sword. He thought about how he and his sister used to argue over the silliest things, and now the two of them were here together, willing to do whatever it took to save one another and get back home. He tried to picture what his parents would be doing at that moment, whether they would be worried, or whether they'd not even noticed their children were missing, like in one of those stories about Narnia where time moves differently between the real world and the fantasy one.

'I want to go home,' he murmured.

'Be brave, User,' Steve said. 'Keep your chin up.'

They walked for about an hour in the direction of the sun. They were beginning to get tired, but

Steve said the village lay just a little further ahead, and they soon discovered he was right. Arthur spotted a blocky tower rising high into the sky. Several lit torches blazed from its roof. Steve explained that they served as a landmark so people didn't get lost, and they also helped to keep away monsters that didn't like the light.

The village started to take shape before Arthur's eyes. There were several grey blocks, some enclosures, and there were mobs pacing around the place. Scattered around were an assortment of animals: cows, chickens, goats, pigs, and even a few cats. It looked pretty much the same as everything else in the Overworld: small pixelated squares, some of them walking around and making noises.

'This is the village where I was born,' said Steve. 'Welcome to Steve's village.'

Arthur nearly laughed out loud when he heard the warrior talking about himself in the third person, but he held his tongue and kept walking until they reached the village. It was good to see a sign of life, even if it wasn't human. This was much better than monsters blowing up in the dead of night. It felt like there was nothing to fear here – it was almost idyllic.

They reached the entrance to the village and came upon a message written on a wooden arch.

THE BEST LIFE IN THE OVERWORLD.

CATS FOR SALE OR HIRE.

'Hello, Steve,' said a voice from nearby. 'Long time no see.'

The siblings turned to the new arrival. He wore a turquoise shirt and purple trousers, and his eyes were two blue dots in his square head. He looked just like the warrior who had rescued them in the forest.

Steve smiled. 'Hello, Steve!' he said. 'I missed you too.'

At those words, Arthur turned to stare at all the passers-by moving around the village. He finally clocked the truth – Steve hadn't been speaking about himself in third person when he had said that they were at Steve's village. Everyone here was identical – they were *all* Steve!

'Right, that's it,' Arthur said, taking a deep breath. 'I think I must have gone mad.'

And that was their first experience of Steve's village.

CHAPTER 8

OLD STEVE

Arthur had started off thinking of the silver-armoured warrior as Steve, so he decided that the others would have to be Steve One, Steve Two and so on. The *original* Steve said they had to keep going because they needed to look for someone called Old Steve who could tell them more about the Diamond Sword. Walking around and seeing all the identical mobs going about their business, Arthur couldn't help but feel a little freaked out. He was also aware that he and his sister were the new kids in town, and the only humans too, so all eyes were on them.

'It's been many a year since we last saw you, Steve,' said Steve One. 'We didn't even know whether you were alive or dead!'

The warrior smiled. 'I needed to get away from it all,' he replied. 'The years of fighting have made it hard for me to settle in a community. I am a warrior, brother; I'm driven by the call of the wild. Please, lead us to Old Steve – only he can help us now.'

Punk-Princess166 laughed out loud. 'Has he always sounded as self-important as he does now?' she asked.

Steve One nodded. 'Steve always had dreams of grandeur – ever since he was a child everyone thought he was a bit snobbish.'

Steve looked offended and lifted his sword fiercely, but everyone just burst out laughing, so eventually he lowered his sword and began to laugh too.

And so they walked through the village, one Steve greeting another. It was perfectly peaceful, as if no one here had heard about the Red King and the monsters under his command. All around them the village was quiet and idyllic.

'We're nearly there,' said Steve One. 'Old Steve has been feeling rather weak lately, so he stays indoors most days.'

Arthur looked ahead to the tiny, red-roofed

stone house they were approaching. Sheep were grazing on the land nearby. Their fleeces were unusual colours: yellow, blue, green and purple. Arthur discovered from his companions that in the Overworld sheep could be dyed different colours – one way that the Overworld was better than Earth.

'Old Steve awaits you,' said Steve One. Apparently, although the Users' arrival had been foretold, most mobs had never expected it to really happen.

Steve One led them towards the door and knocked. A few seconds later, a husky voice was heard.

'Let the Users in, Steve. I have waited many years for this moment.'

Arthur stepped forward and pushed the door open, followed by Punk-Princess166 and the two Steves.

He smelled smoke with a hint of cinnamon, and after a bout of coughing he blinked his eyes. The room was barer than Steve's: just a bed, a fruit basket and a candle that was filling the house with smoke. Sitting on the bed, nodding his square head slightly, was Old Steve. He was almost identical to the other Steves, except for his white beard.

'Look,' said Punk-Princess166. 'An old Steve! I never saw anything like that while playing Minecraft.'

'Be polite to the old man,' said Steve One. 'He's very important in our community.'

Old Steve laughed. 'Don't be so hard on her, Steve,' he said. 'I must look as odd to her as she does to us.'

The thoughts in Arthur's head were rather different. *Where do all these Steves come from?* he wondered. *Were they hatched out of eggs or grown from seeds? Have they been created by some sort of divine programmer from the Minecraft world?*

He had more questions than he could deal with. The Overworld was turning out to be a very tricky place to get your head around. But Arthur tried not to get distracted, and to remember the reason why they'd come to this place.

'We need help, Old Steve,' he said. 'We need to get out of this world and go back home –'

'And to do so you will need Herobrine's sword.' The old man cut him short. 'The mythical Diamond Sword. I know everything . . .'

Arthur was filled with sudden hope. Perhaps

there was a way to get out of this situation!

'Can you help us?' he asked.

The old man scratched his head, took a deep breath and said, 'I can't.'

They were all taken aback by the answer. Arthur and Punk-Princess166 could not believe their ears. Even with their limited expressions, Arthur could see that Steve and Steve One were stunned too – their eyes closed until they turned into lines and their rectangular arms moved up and down.

'Please, Old Steve, help us,' pleaded Steve.

'No,' repeated the old man, smiling broadly and swinging his legs.

Arthur closed his eyes and sighed. Then he opened them again as he heard footsteps, and a familiar, bossy voice.

'Oldie,' said Punk-Princess166, walking towards the old man. 'We've come a long way to ask you for help and all you can say is "no"? I think it's in your interest too that the Red King is defeated.'

'No.'

'Why can't you help us?'

'No.'

Arthur swore then, and turned his back on Old Steve. He had run out of patience; this was just another dead end. Arthur left the house as fast as he could, retracing his steps on the path they'd taken to get there.

The square sun was going down and the sky was growing darker. The Overworld's last minutes of calm would soon be over.

This is so frustrating! Arthur thought. He knew what they had to do, but had no idea how to do it. He hated the Overworld, every bit of it, every square of that world of blocks and every useless mob roaming about in it. He hated the Steves as much as he hated creepers and spiders, so much so that he almost wished the Red King would destroy the whole stupid place.

'Noobie!' shouted Punk-Princess166 from right behind him. 'Wait a bit. You can't leave the village – it'll be nightfall soon!'

'I don't care!'

'Don't be silly. We've got to think about what we're going to do. I'm your sister, aren't I? You have to listen to me.'

Arthur stopped abruptly. 'You can stay here making your mind up about what to do,' he snapped. 'But my patience is wearing thin. I hate every single thing about this world. Unlike you, I don't love being here.'

Nothing else was said. In a split second Punk-Princess166 reached him, and Arthur felt a slap across his face that could be heard across the village. His sister's hand hit his face so hard and so abruptly that he could do nothing but stand still in shock.

'You idiot,' she said in a cold, low voice. 'You really don't know anything about me, do you? We don't even look like brother and sister. Do you really think I'd like to spend my whole life here and never see our world again? Only you could think something like that. I want to get back home too, but running off and throwing a tantrum isn't going to solve anything.'

Several Steves stood stunned, witnessing the scene. Arthur put his hand on his cheek, where he had been hit. He felt his skin burning, but that wasn't what hurt the most. The shame was worse. He was grateful that darkness was falling to hide him. He could not believe how insensitive he had been, thinking his sister was just having fun, that everything was all right and that she didn't care about her family back in the real world.

'I'm sorry,' he finally said, his voice shaking. 'I should never have said that.'

Punk-Princess166 turned. 'It would be wrong not to forgive an idiot, idiot.'

Arthur knew exactly what his sister's expression would be as she said those words. He tried to think of a clever response, but before he could say anything, they heard a horrible noise, like the cry of a pained or grieving animal played out through a megaphone. It was such a terrifying noise that it sent all the villagers running into the shelter of their homes.

'We need to get out of here, Users!' someone called.

It was warrior Steve, who had just arrived. He wielded his sword ready to fight, but when they saw what lay at the village entrance, they all knew that his sword wouldn't be enough. All they could see were three metres of pitch-black darkness.

The creature rose as tall as a lamppost, with long, thin arms and purple eyes that shone as brightly as its sharp teeth. It took long strides, and a red ring of light glowed around its neck. The creature set its eyes on them and howled again, ready to charge.

Then, with her lip quaking and an expression of dread on her face, Punk-Princess166 let out a single word.

'Enderman.'

CHAPTER 9

THE ENDERMAN'S ATTACK

Dread comes in many shapes and colours, and all of them are horrible. It doesn't matter whether it's that childhood fear of what dwells in the dark or what lies hidden under the bed, or whether it's strangers in the street – they can all be scary. But there is a particular kind of dread that's different from all of these: the fear we feel when we face a monster that's real, one that could actually hurt us or even tear us apart. This was what Arthur and his sister felt when they saw the giant enderman with its long arms and huge teeth.

'Run!' shouted Arthur. 'We need to get out of here!'

Punk-Princess166 stood still. 'That wouldn't help,' she said. 'It's already seen us. It's seen all of us.'

Arthur looked at the monster, and in that exact moment the enderman disappeared. There was a deafening noise, as if a giant whip had lashed the air; it was so loud that everyone covered their ears with their hands as a purple glow appeared before them. For many, this purple glow was the last thing they saw.

'Where did it go?' someone shouted.

'Run into the tunnels!' ordered someone else. 'We can hide there!'

The enderman suddenly materialized behind Arthur, his sister and Steve. It just appeared there, as though it had been there all along. It stretched out its arms, caught up one of the Steves cowering before it and hurled its victim against a house nearby. A pixel blast followed, and the Steve that had been attacked was gone.

'My arm!' someone else screamed. 'It's eaten my arm!'

Arthur held Punk-Princess166's hand tight and pulled her away from the monster. Steve's village was being destroyed. The dead and the injured were piling up, and around them rubble crumbled to the ground. It was like a scene from a disaster movie. Everyone tried to run for shelter, but they couldn't work out what the enderman would do next because it kept appearing and disappearing so quickly. Nowhere was safe.

'We have to get out of here,' said Steve the warrior. 'The enderman will go on until everything is destroyed.'

Punk-Princess166 stumbled as she tried to keep up with Arthur and Steve. Arthur could hear the sound of houses being knocked down and the screams of people losing their homes, their loved ones and their lives. But they had no choice – they had to keep running. They were just children – what use would they be against a senseless monster which attacked everything in its way? As they ran their feet beat hard on the ground, and for a moment Arthur really believed they would manage to get away from Steve's village. But he was wrong.

'Watch out!' Punk-Princess166 screamed.

First came the noise: the sound of a cracking whip. Then a beam of purple light – and the enemy was on top of them. Three metres of black horror with a gaping mouth.

Arthur swore, but nobody heard him amid the chaos. The enderman stretched out its arm and punched Arthur hard. There was no way to escape. He just shut his eyes and waited to be hit again.

'I'm sorry, Mallu, I really am sorry, but I won't be able to save you,' he said. 'We're never going to get home.'

A gust of wind surged and ruffled Arthur's hair; he heard someone falling hard on to the ground next to him.

Opening his eyes, Arthur saw Old Steve lying beside him, covered in bruises. There was a smile on his face, as if he got a kick out of what was happening.

Arthur and Punk-Princess166 rushed to help the old man, kneeling down beside him as Steve fought the monster with his sword.

'Why did you protect Arthur?' asked Punk-Princess166. 'You said you weren't going to help us.'

Old Steve's sword lay by Arthur's foot, just a few centimetres away, but all Arthur could do was stare at the old man on the ground. He felt sick. His skin was hot, as if his blood was burning in his veins.

Old Steve spat out blood before answering Punk-Princess166's question.

'You asked if I could help you,' he managed. 'If I could . . . help you . . . and I can't. You are the Users heralded in an ancient prophecy, and I am just an old man. Your mission is to find the mythical legend's sword and defeat the Red King. Users, every hope we have of saving the Overworld lies with you. Follow . . . follow . . . the sun.'

Arthur went to shake the old man, but his body had already shattered into thousands of pixels, which were spreading all over the ground. Old Steve was dead. Arthur wished he had understood what Old Steve had meant earlier. It wasn't just about getting back home – it was also about saving the world from a boy who wanted to play at being king. He and Punk-Princess166 were the only ones who could save the Overworld. Arthur didn't want to see people getting hurt any more, whether they were humans or mobs. Minecraft was just a game, but, somehow, real living things existed in the

Overworld. Never again would Arthur stand still when everything around him was falling apart.

'Over here, you stupid monster!' he shouted, straightening up. 'Enderman, you moron, look at me! Aren't I the one you're after? I'm a User!' Arthur shouted, trying to draw the enderman his way.

The monster, which had a Steve caught in its hand, flung its victim aside and teleported to right in front of Arthur. They faced each other. Nobody moved. Then, in the stillness, a voice spoke.

The strange, calm voice came from the enderman's mouth, but there was no doubt it wasn't the monster speaking.

'Good evening, User,' the voice said. 'I am the Red King, he who rules over everything in the Overworld.'

Everyone stood still; the villagers had frozen as soon as they heard the Red King's voice. Even though his voice was just conveyed through the enderman, they could feel the enemy's presence. No one dared to speak – except for one person.

'You're an idiot,' said Punk-Princess166. 'A big fat idiot, as big as an elephant.'

The enderman burst out laughing. 'What a cheeky girl we've got here,' said the Red King.

'Nice to meet you too,' Punk-Princess166 said.

Arthur remained silent, picturing the kind of person who could control a monster like the enderman and use it as a puppet. But that didn't matter – all that mattered was that this was the person who had hurt hundreds of Steves.

'I want you to let us leave the Overworld,' Arthur said carefully. 'We don't want to cause any problems.'

The enderman nodded. 'Sure, I can get you out of here.'

'All right, then take us back home, or . . .'

'Or what? There's nothing you can do to stop an enderman. Didn't you see what one can do? I have a huge army. But there *is* a way for the three of us to all get what we want.'

Arthur took a deep breath.

'Don't believe him,' said Steve. 'He's a liar.'

But Arthur paid no attention to his friend. 'Please, just tell us what you want,' he said.

The Red King's reply was so awful that as soon as he spoke Punk-Princess166 began to swear at him and Steve started pleading with the Users not to agree to the king's request.

'All I want is the sword that defeated Herobrine,' said the Red King. His voice was firm and ruthless-sounding. Arthur wasn't surprised that the Red King wanted something from them in return for sending them home, but he had never expected his enemy to make *that* request. 'The same sword you no doubt intended to use against me. I can only access the portal I have to your world if the sword is brought to City 01 and handed over to me.'

'How can you expect us to find a sword we don't even know exists?' Arthur said angrily.

'You're Users,' replied the Red King. 'I'm sure you'll manage somehow. I'll wait for you in City 01. Don't be too long.'

Arthur stepped forward, but then the enderman disappeared in a purple cloud just as he had arrived, leaving behind the destruction and the many dead and injured. The scent of burning wood rose into the sky, and the wail of those who had been left behind rang out across the night.

There and then, surrounded by all that chaos and

destruction, Arthur swore to himself that he would find the Diamond Sword, destroy the Red King and get his sister back home.

'Let's find that damn sword,' he said.

'And hand it over to the king?' said Steve. 'Are you mad?'

'No, Steve,' Arthur said. 'We're going to find the sword and defeat the Red King, no matter what.'

PART THREE: Endermen

By Punk-Princess166

If you're looking for someone you definitely don't want to invite to your birthday party, I'd say an enderman would be top of your list. These creatures are several metres tall, with long arms and purple eyes. They are so deadly that if you come across them my only advice would be this: in the name of Herobrine, RUN!

They can travel from one place to another in an instant; some studies have suggested that this skill comes from the pearls they have instead of hearts, known as ender pearls. An enderman hates it when you look at it – and believe me, it will always know when you're looking. This is one of the key traits I've discovered about endermen.

These monsters are also notorious kleptomaniacs, which means they steal things they don't actually need. So it's pretty common to find an enderman taking parts of people's houses when they're not looking. If anyone tells you that part of your house or your crop is gone, then beware: you have a visitor lurking nearby.

And good luck.

CHAPTER 10

GO AHEAD, USERS!

Steve's village had been totally destroyed by the enderman under the control of the Red King. Mobs looked at what was left of their crops and their friends, unable to comprehend what had happened. It took over an hour for everyone to come out of their hiding places and for their wailing to fade away. But the night had not ended yet, and the Steves knew that their grief and mourning would have to be delayed until the coming dawn.

'Remember how I said you were lucky not to have met an enderman before?' Punk-Princess166 said to her brother.

Arthur looked at her. She seemed tired, and, despite his attempts to cheer her up, there was no trace of a smile on her face. She had found Arthur sitting on the rubble of Old Steve's house, thinking about what the old mob had sacrificed, and how they were going to find the sword.

Steve the warrior, along with some volunteers, was combing the area looking for a clue. *That sword must be really powerful*, Arthur thought. *A whole legend has grown up around it, and it's caught the attention of the Red King too.* He shifted to let his sister sit down next to him.

'Well, I know a lot more now,' he said to her. 'I wouldn't like to imagine what else might be lurking around here.'

'You'd better not – it could be even worse.' Punk-Princess166 put her hands in her pockets and looked up at the sky. 'The Overworld is an odd place, Noobie. Things don't turn out the way you hope they will here, and if we want to survive we need to learn how to deal with that.'

'You used to spend hours playing Minecraft. Tell me – what can we do? Those millions of virtual hours must come in handy, surely.'

Punk-Princess166 nodded. 'I spent hours playing

Minecraft because I had nothing else to do,' she said. 'You hardly spent any time with me, and neither did Mum and Dad. You were always their favourite. They didn't care about me. So, sure, I played a lot, but it was only because nobody in the real world cared about me.'

Arthur's face felt hot as he listened to his sister. He thought of all the things he'd said in the past, not realizing how she really felt.

'Hey!' shouted Steve, coming to join them. 'I think I know what we have to do.'

Arthur stared at the warrior as he approached them. He looked exhausted, his body covered in dirt from head to toe, and he carried a scroll of paper in his hand.

'I'm all ears,' replied Punk-Princess166. 'We could really do with some good news right now.'

Steve unrolled the giant scroll and showed it to his friends. It was a map of the whole region and its surroundings: the forest where Arthur and Punk-Princess166 had met and Steve's village both fell within a region labelled *Territories*. Steve pointed to a spot inside the Territories, where the map read:

The Priestess's Temple. It lay on top of a hill above a wide river. Or at least that's what it looked like to Arthur.

'How's this going to help us?' asked Arthur. 'The old man said we had to follow the sun, not go to some priestess's temple.'

Steve wasn't put off by Arthur's question. 'The temple is on the way to the sun,' Steve told them excitedly. 'The priestess is a powerful mob who knows the answers to many questions. People go to her temple searching for advice and wisdom, young man. If anyone knows where Herobrine's sword is, it's her. That's where we should be heading right now.'

Arthur stayed quiet, trying to think of a way to avoid taking any unnecessary risks. Every part of the Overworld was dangerous. How could they reach the priestess without bumping into any of the creepers or endermen roaming through the night? *Damn it!* Arthur thought. They needed to get out of that place as soon as they could.

Arthur rose and looked further ahead, where the first rays of dawn were beginning to touch the trees in the fields; a sad, reluctant sunlight that seemed to reflect the mood of the village and every Steve now attempting to rebuild his home.

'So I think we know what we're going to do next,' said Punk-Princess166. 'Standing here isn't going to help – the Red King won't be defeated unless we *do* something.'

'You're right,' said Steve. 'We need to get back on the road and take advantage of the sunlight for as long as we can.'

Arthur nodded, agreeing with Steve and his sister. The only way to defeat the Red King was to follow any lead, no matter how hopeless it might seem. With a sigh, he made up his mind: they would go to the priestess's, and even if that didn't lead to anything, they would keep on trying until they found a way to get back home.

'You're right,' he said. 'We should get ready to set off. I'd love to be able to help all the Steves rebuild their village, but we're running out of time.'

'Exactly, Noobie,' said Punk-Princess166. 'You've finally figured out how to use your brain – congratulations.'

Arthur made a face at her and rubbed his eyes, a sure sign that he was tired. He shook his head and decided to put the rest of the plan into action. If they were going to reach the temple before nightfall, then there was no time to waste.

Their next step was to ask Steve One for help. He was looking after the injured in a makeshift tent; he had been wounded on his head and right arm, but he was not as badly hurt as some of the others.

'Hey,' Steve the warrior called as they approached Steve One. 'How are you?'

Arthur had always found it weird the way people ask how you are even after a tragedy, when the answer is never going to be positive. Arthur's theory about the answer to Steve's question was confirmed as he reached the mob: Steve One was wrapped in dirty bandages and looked exhausted, as though all his pixels ached.

'The worst is over,' he answered. 'Most people managed to escape, and the dead have already been buried.'

There was silence.

'I'm sorry to hear that,' replied Steve the warrior.

'We will make the Red King pay for everything he has done.'

'That's all I want,' said Steve One. 'Revenge for what he has done to Old Steve and all the others who have suffered.'

Punk-Princess166 stepped forward and looked at the mob. She wore a serious expression; her hands rested on her waist and her chin was up.

'I know this is an awful time,' she said. 'I am so sorry about what's happened. But we need your help. We won't be able to stay here long – the Overworld is getting more and more dangerous for us. We need weapons and supplies for our journey. Steve, would you be able to arrange that for us?'

The mob looked back at her. He was exhausted, as they all were, so he took a while to answer, and when he did, he answered only with a single nod. Then he rose and went to fetch the things Punk-Princess166 had asked for.

It took about an hour to get it all ready. The villagers brought all they could to help. It was a slow job, but by the end they had all the provisions they needed: the two wooden swords, some torches, rucksacks, and a wide range of food such as corn, cake, sugar cane and some loaves of bread. It might not seem much, bearing in mind the conditions under which they'd be travelling in that dangerous world, but it would be enough to get them to the priestess's temple.

'It's not a huge amount, I'm afraid, but it's all we can afford to give you,' Steve One said. A small crowd of people had gathered around the Users. 'I hope, for all our sakes, that your mission is successful.'

Arthur hoped so too. He didn't even want to imagine what would happen if it all went wrong.

'It will be, my brother,' answered Steve the warrior. 'I am certain.'

Punk-Princess166 draped an arm over Arthur's shoulders.

'Don't you worry,' she said, 'we're going to kick the Red King's butt so hard he'll apologize straight away.'

This was the only time Steve One seemed to smile – just a slight twitch at the corner of his lips. There was nothing else left to say or do. Nobody spoke; Arthur, Punk-Princess166 and Steve just walked among the villagers who made way for them in silence so the uncertain heroes could pass through on their way to save all of their lives.

And so, as the square sun began to shine high in the sky, the Users and the warrior stepped out of the village. The world unfolded before them, and every centimetre of the Overworld hinted to them that they were now walking into the greatest danger they had ever faced.

CHAPTER 11

THE TELEPHONE BOOTH

They walked for over an hour in silence. Around them there was nothing but the plain, with trees scattered across the fields, and mountains far off on the horizon. They walked fast, but not so fast that they'd get tired – they had to save some energy for the night shift.

Arthur gazed across the landscape. The Overworld was not completely unattractive, now that he wasn't fighting for his life and could take a look at it a little more comfortably. There were so many different colours; it was such a vast space that he could see the woodlands stretch right to the horizon and out of sight. During the day, it was peaceful and quiet; there was a warm breeze, and every block was in its proper place. A part of Arthur could understand why the place appealed to his sister – it gave her the freedom to change things, to put them together in a way that made sense to no one else but her. It was a place where her parents never shouted at her, and where nothing was ever truly wrong, even if monsters roamed about at night. Everything was under her control.

He stared at his sister. For the first time he noticed how much she had grown up. Her face was slimmer and her arms weren't as podgy as they used to be. In fact, she was now in better shape than him – probably better able to run away from monsters. Arthur knew he ran awkwardly and got out of breath quickly – a classic example of someone who knew a lot more about rap music and Japanese cartoons than physical exercise.

'Hey, idiot,' Punk-Princess166 said, catching his eye. 'You're too quiet. That usually means you're thinking about something stupid.'

Arthur shrugged. 'According to you, I only ever think stupid things,' he answered. 'I was actually just thinking how grown up you've become.'

She paused to retie the laces on her trainers. She was covered in dirt and scratches. Arthur remembered that she had been in the Overworld longer than him; she'd been here in those first few minutes when he'd still been in the real world.

'It happens,' said Punk-Princess166. She looked a little puzzled at what her brother had said. 'I tried to avoid it, but there's only one Peter Pan.'

'What's Peter Pan?' asked Steve, who had kept quiet until then. 'Is that a profession from the world you come from?'

'No,' Punk-Princess166 said. 'He's just a silly boy who kidnaps children and puts them in danger. He uses his age as an excuse for it.'

'Then I think it's a good thing that there's only one of him,' Steve concluded after a pause.

Arthur's thoughts had already drifted off elsewhere when something caught his eye. At first he didn't know what it was – something was glowing from far away, something that seemed out of place in the woods. He nudged his sister's shoulder and pointed in that direction, about twenty metres away.

'What do you think that is, Steve?' asked Arthur. 'It doesn't look like anything I've seen in the Overworld up until now.'

'It could be a trap set by the Red King,' Steve replied. 'Ever since he turned up here, lots of odd things have appeared – creatures and artefacts we can hardly understand.'

'They're *mods*, Steve,' replied Punk-Princess166. 'Changes he's making in the Overworld.'

Arthur approached the light, warily raising the wooden sword he had been given by Steve the warrior. He could now see the glowing object more clearly, its shape becoming more apparent with every step he took.

Arthur glanced to check if Steve and his sister were as shocked as he was when he realized what he was seeing: the straight red lines of a telephone box. It was one of the old-fashioned British sort that tourists took photos of. It looked kind of out of place in the Overworld.

'It could be worse,' Punk-Princess166 said. 'Anything that isn't an enderman is a bonus right now.'

As Arthur stared at the telephone box, something occurred to him: what if he could go inside and make a phone call home? The booth wasn't made up of pixels like everything else was – perhaps its origin could be traced back to their own world.

Punk-Princess166 must have been thinking the same, because suddenly she broke into a run towards the booth. Steve and Arthur followed. Arthur thought about calling his parents or even the police – someone had to be able to find a way to help them. He ran as fast as he could towards the booth, his rucksack jolting and rattling on his back.

'Hang on, Users!' shouted Steve. 'It could be a trap!'

Arthur ignored his friend's advice and squeezed into the box with his sister. Arthur lifted the phone and dialled their home phone number with his other hand. He pressed his ear hard against the receiver to make sure he would hear any sounds, however faint they might be.

He made out some clicks, and then a long silence. Then, suddenly, a female voice spoke.

'I'm sorry, we can't connect your call. Please try again later.' The message was repeated again and again, the voice flat and expressionless.

It took a moment for the siblings to grasp what the words meant.

'It doesn't work,' said Arthur. 'Nothing works properly here.'

They tried all the phone numbers they knew, all the emergency numbers and even the phone number of the Chinese restaurant on the corner of the building where they lived. But every time they got the same answer in that faceless, uncompromising voice. Yet another frustration of the Overworld. Arthur punched his fist against the side of the booth and then pushed his way out, leaving his sister – and a crack in the glass – behind.

'Did you find what you were looking for?' asked Steve.

'It was a waste of time.' Arthur didn't bother to hide his frustration. 'Nothing makes sense here. This place sucks! I wish I'd never found that stupid floppy disc.'

The mob put his square hand on Arthur's

shoulder; his touch was gentle, despite the heavy gauntlet he wore.

'Don't lose patience, User. Even the very worst problems have a solution. Trust me – I've been through many wars and many dangers. I have plenty of experience of these things.'

Arthur sighed, the anger suddenly draining out of him.

'I know, Steve, but it's hard when nothing makes any sense. Every time we seem to be getting closer to a solution, everything gets more muddled.'

The warrior smiled and looked away. Punk-Princess166 approached them, moving slowly, as if she'd also given up trying after their failure in the telephone box. She scratched her head and kicked little stones on the road – a sure sign that she was upset. She hitched up her rucksack and said nothing as she joined them. They all knew that the best they could do was keep searching for the temple.

'Let's make a move,' she said. 'This is just a waste of time.'

Arthur nodded and began walking. It was just a useless telephone. It didn't make any sense that it was there, but there was no point dwelling on it. They had to find Herobrine's sword and get out of that world. If it really was as powerful as the legend suggested, the sword would allow them to defeat the Red King and return to the real world.

Arthur was daydreaming about that possibility when something jolted him back to reality – a tinkling, ringing sound like a bell. Or rather, like . . . a telephone!

'Users?' called Steve.

'I can hear it too!' Arthur replied before Steve could say anything else.

The three of them stared at the telephone box as it went on ringing. And then they sprang into action – there was no time to waste! They bolted towards the box, their armour and equipment rattling as they ran. Dust rose from the ground as though a herd of elephants was stampeding past.

'Quick!' shouted Punk-Princess166.

Arthur was the first one into the telephone booth. He grabbed the receiver so tightly his veins showed through the skin and his fingers looked like claws. He placed it against his ear and waited in silence, his heart pounding, his breath coming fast. Then, finally, he heard a voice from the other side. His heart leaped.

'Have you seen Herobrine?'

Arthur froze and stared at his sister. 'Who's speaking?' he asked.

Like rising music, the voice kept on speaking, as though Arthur hadn't said anything at all.

'Herobrine is here. Herobrine wants his sword. Herobrine is here. Herobrine is dead. Herobrine is here. Have you seen Herobrine? At his home in the Nether, the dead Herobrine awaits. Herobrine is dreaming.'

'Hello?' Arthur said.

Then the voice went silent with a *snap*, and the voice they'd heard earlier returned. 'I'm sorry, we can't connect your call. Please try again later.'

They tried pressing all the keys on the keypad but nothing worked. The only thing they knew for sure was that there was more to all this than met the eye. Like an arm that reaches through the shadows to catch you unawares, someone from the darkness was trying to make contact. Some nameless person seemed to be working for Herobrine . . . even after his death.

'What happened?' asked Punk-Princess166.

Arthur said nothing. *Maybe*, he thought, *Herobrine isn't as dead as people think*. He shivered, and his hope wavered at the very thought of it.

CONCEPTS OF THE OVERWORLD

PART FOUR: Redstone

By Punk-Princess166

Redstone is my favourite thing in the Overworld. Or, at least, it was until that so-called Red King ruined it for me.

Redstone acts like electrical energy in the digital world; it can make trains run, and power even more complex machines than that; it can enhance your creativity so you can make things you would once have thought impossible in Minecraft.

If you want a submarine or an army tank, you will need redstone to make it run. The cool thing is that it's a sustainable source of energy that doesn't destroy the world or pollute the air. It would be amazing if there was redstone in the real world – maybe then the environment wouldn't be so messed up!

It was only when he discovered how valuable redstone actually was that the Red King decided to mine as much of it as he could, and to steal the redstone that people already had.

That guy is such a jerk.

CHAPTER 12

ON THE ROAD

They set off again. When Arthur told them what the voice had said in the telephone booth, Steve and Punk-Princess166 were completely bewildered. Steve kept asking Arthur to repeat the words over and over again, so that they could analyse and pick apart every phrase.

'You don't understand,' Steve said. His voice was hoarse and distant. 'This is much bigger than the Red King and his creepers causing havoc. I grew up hearing stories about Herobrine. The Overworld still exists only because Herobrine has been banished to the Nether. Otherwise he would have destroyed it.'

Arthur looked up and realized the day was

ending. They needed to find shelter before the monsters came out at nightfall. As they walked, Punk-Princess166 tried to calm Steve down.

'It could just be a trick by the Red King to scare people away,' she said. 'Everybody has heard stories about Herobrine where I come from, but I've never met a player who has actually seen him.'

'The Overworld isn't a game,' answered Steve. 'And Herobrine isn't a legend. He's real.'

Arthur stared at the warrior. Steve had never looked frightened before – not when he was fighting against the spiders or even when the enderman had appeared – but now he looked terrified.

Perhaps the telephone call was a warning. What if it had been a sign that finding Herobrine's sword might not be the right thing to do? Maybe they should stop before it was too late and they had to face a much bigger threat than a greedy king.

'What do you think we should do, Steve?' Arthur asked. 'I don't think we can go back now. Mallu and I will never get home unless we find the sword and defeat the Red King. We knew it'd be risky from the very beginning – that's not changed.'

'Nothing is more important than preventing Herobrine's return,' Steve said.

'Getting back home is,' Arthur told him, and then he turned away and kept walking.

'You can't go on as if nothing has happened,' Steve said.

'Hey, Noobie, wait for us,' Punk-Princess166 called as Arthur kept walking away from them.

Steve was obviously upset; he grumbled and then fell silent. But the truth was, Arthur had made his mind up. After everything he had heard about Herobrine, of course he felt scared, but he was willing to do pretty much anything to escape from this world – even if that meant awakening a terrible monster and fighting against him with nothing but a wooden sword. He didn't *want* to wake Herobrine – he knew that Steve and all his friends in the village had done everything they could to help him and his sister, and if the stories were true, then Herobrine might well slay them all. He didn't want that – of course he didn't. But he couldn't just give up without trying. He had to do all he could.

'I think you pushed too hard with Steve,' Punk-Princess166 said, when they were far enough away for the mob not to be able to hear them. 'I want to get home too, but this is Steve's world.'

Arthur put his hands in his pockets, upset about the whole situation. 'I know, but once we get back home, we can help them,' he answered. 'If we're outside the world and playing the game, we can reprogram it or something. Maybe we'll be able to just . . . get rid of the Red King by pressing delete.'

Punk-Princess166 smiled. Arthur could tell she thought he was being an idiot – that was usually what that particular smile meant.

'You really don't get it, do you?'

'What?'

'This isn't a game,' she said. 'What happens here is real, and each and every villager is real. Look at Steve and the others we have met so far. They are complex people with their own unique skills; they can suffer and die. If you're playing Minecraft and you die, you turn up again somewhere else, but that isn't what seems to happen here. There are differences between this Overworld and the world I know from the game. It's like the game is the carbon copy of this world; maybe we came through it and landed in the actual digital world.'

The sun was going down, leaving a trace of orange in the sky. According to Arthur's calculations, there was about an hour of light left, but they needed to hurry if they were going to reach the temple before nightfall.

'Do you mean we aren't inside the game? You think we're in another universe?' asked Arthur, more confused than ever.

In a rare display of affection, Arthur's sister put her arm round him. She'd never have done that at home – or if their lives hadn't been at risk.

'Exactly,' she said. 'Think about it. If there are thousands of parallel worlds, chances are there is a world where the Overworld and the Nether are real – where Steve is as much of a real person as we are.'

It was a totally crazy idea, but Arthur couldn't help considering it. Maybe he was on the other side of a mirror, in some kind of Wonderland. If so, it was definitely one where the queen wanted to chop your head off, not one with a friendly white rabbit to guide you.

'Where did you get all that parallel-universe stuff from?' Arthur asked his sister.

Punk-Princess166 raised her chin. 'Unlike you, I like to find out about things,' she said. She fixed her hair before continuing. 'I read somewhere that Stephen Hawking has said that in an alternative universe, Zayn may still be part of One Direction.'

'Wait. Are you saying that your whole theory is based on a scientist's joke about a *boy band*?'

Punk-Princess166 shrugged her shoulders. She looked relaxed now, and in a better mood. 'It's better than no explanation at all,' she said. 'Hey, maybe there's even a boy band in the Overworld: The Backstreet Mobs, maybe? Believe me, they'd be a huge hit.'

'Please don't tell any more jokes like that,' Arthur said, 'this one is already too painful!'

Punk-Princess166 laughed and opened her mouth to reply, but she was interrupted by a whistle from Steve. He was still upset with them, obviously.

Maybe he thinks a whistle is all we deserve, Arthur thought.

'I think we're in luck,' said Punk-Princess166. 'Steve has found a shelter.'

The warrior pointed to a small stone construction, about five metres long by five metres wide, with a tiny window and a small wooden door. Distracted by his sister, Arthur hadn't noticed the small shelter across the plains, but it would be a perfect little hiding place where they could stay for the night. Already the sun was giving way to the square moon, alone up there in the sky, without even a tiny star for company.

'Do you think it's safe, Steve?' Arthur asked.

'Safer than awakening Herobrine,' the warrior replied. 'I don't think there's anything in there that could destroy this world.'

'Come on,' Arthur said. 'Don't be like that.'

Steve just turned his back on Arthur and opened the door. The three of them were welcomed by a musty smell – it seemed like no one had lived in that room for years.

The bedroom was bare – there was no bed or

chair, just plain dark walls made of cobblestone. Punk-Princess166 pulled a torch from her rucksack and lit it; the glow blinded them briefly, but eventually revealed a crimson message high up on one of the walls.

THE RED KING LIVES HERE

CHAPTER 13

INTO THE DARKNESS

Arthur had read in a magazine that the human brain can interpret an image in just thirteen milliseconds. But sometimes the mind takes longer to process things and to really believe what it's seeing. Such as the fact they were now at the Red King's house.

They stood still, staring around the mouldy little room as though they had discovered a lost kingdom. Even Steve seemed to forget that he was upset and moved nearer to Arthur and PunkPrincess166.

'I think we'd better find somewhere else to stay the night,' said the warrior. 'We need to get out of here before the Red King turns up.'

Punk-Princess166 waggled her finger, pacing around the room and scrutinizing every bit of it.

'He won't come back here,' she said. 'We're at his first house. His spawn point is probably around here.'

'Spawn point?' Arthur asked. 'Remember, I don't know anything about this world, unlike you two.'

Noises floated in from outside. Some were unfamiliar, but some Arthur knew all too well – the blast of a creeper exploding, for instance. He watched his sister fix a torch into a hole in the wall.

'Keep up, Noobie,' she said. 'The spawn point is the place you start from when you first enter the game. It's where you're born – your point of origin. New players usually build their homes near to their spawn point so that they can survive their first night in the Overworld. After that, they become more daring and start venturing out to mine and to find new things.'

It was Steve's turn to ask a question now. He was staring out the window, tapping one foot on the floor as if he was keeping the beat to a song they couldn't hear. 'So this means that the Red King –

that evil being who rules half the world – started out right here, in this shack near my village?'

'Probably, Steve,' Punk-Princess166 replied. 'Probably. But judging by the message on the wall, he was always ambitious. A kid who saw himself as the master of the world, I guess. He's just an idiot, like players from the world I come from who prefer to destroy other players' creations rather than build their own.'

Arthur realized his sister was upset, but not just about the Red King – she was upset about something personal. Obviously they hadn't been close back home, but he did remember a period when she had been bullied at school because of the way she looked. Kids had been sending her horrible texts; their mother had had to go in to the school, and, eventually, his sister had been transferred to another school. Arthur hadn't thought much about it at the time – he'd been more interested in Deafheaven's latest album – but now he wondered what was behind the pranks those kids used to play on his sister, and whether it might have been something really nasty.

'I think I've found something here,' said Steve, catching Arthur's eye. 'Listen – when you tap on this part of the floor it sounds hollow. It might be a . . .'

The warrior was just beneath the window, banging on the floor with his square hand and listening for the echo. He grabbed a stone pickaxe and struck the floor four or five times, until part of it turned into dust and disappeared. Steve edged away and let Arthur and Punk-Princess166 peer into the hole. A wooden ladder led down into the darkness. There were no sounds from below, and there was no trace of light.

'What do you think is down there?' Arthur asked.

'Mines,' volunteered his sister. 'He probably dug tunnels and mined down there while he lived here.'

'I think we should try to go down,' said Steve. 'Perhaps we can find something useful, or even something that might help us understand our enemy.'

Arthur nodded. Grabbing a torch from the wall, he headed down the ladder. Steve and Punk-Princess166 followed, each with a torch in hand, so that they could see the path that lay ahead of them.

There was no sign of life – just a long, grey, endless path.

'Mines,' the girl said. 'Just as I'd suspected. Well, we better keep on walking – maybe he left some weapons and food behind.'

'If we find anything edible, I'm pretty sure it'll be past its sell-by date,' Arthur pointed out.

'Food doesn't have a sell-by date in the Overworld, Noobie – unless it's zombie's flesh, which is already rotten.'

Arthur shook his head in disgust and kept on walking, his footsteps echoing through the long, deserted tunnel. He was claustrophobic – he hated being in small spaces – so he wasn't exactly enjoying exploring the tunnels. He struggled to breathe; his hands shook. Panic was taking over, like water surging from a broken dam. Taking a slow, deep breath, he tried to calm down. He couldn't have a panic attack right now – that would make everything even harder for them all. His panic would have to wait. Maybe when he got out of here he could go and see a psychologist who would help him with all the traumas he'd had to deal with in the Overworld.

'Stay on alert,' said Steve. 'Monsters usually spawn in any tunnel that's dark enough. There could be a creeper or a spider anywhere around here.'

'Thank you very much, Steve,' replied Arthur. 'As if I wasn't scared to death already!'

'You're always scared, brother,' Punk-Princess166 remarked.

'And if you weren't totally insane, you'd be scared too. Fear is nature's safety warning, Mallu. It's a way for her to tell us, "don't do anything silly and get yourself killed".'

They continued along the straight path for over twenty minutes, until finally the tunnel turned left. From that point on, the path descended down hundreds of steps. Arthur thought about all the hard work that must have gone into creating that path – all the hours the Red King had wasted here, alone in the dark.

The path wound on, bits of it crumbling away as they walked. They came upon a few pieces of equipment that had been left behind, broken pickaxes and shovels abandoned after so much heavy work. Punk-Princess166 explained to Arthur that, in Minecraft, people dug in search of precious minerals and metals. The deeper they went, the more they would find – and the greater the risks.

'It could be worse, Users,' said Steve. 'At least the Red King didn't create a labyrinth. I remember a time when a Steve dug so far in all directions that he ended up getting lost.'

'What happened to him?' Arthur asked.

Steve scratched his head before answering. 'Nothing major – he just died. A good thing too. His assets were shared out, and I got his sugar cane, which was just what I needed to make a cake.'

'Steve! Isn't that a little insensitive?' said Punk-Princess166.

'It wasn't like he needed the sugar cane any more. And don't forget that the Red King's actions caused serious inflation in the Overworld. Everything got more expensive. Damn the Red King – before he was around I could exchange two hens for a whole cake! Now you need a lot more than that if you want any villager to give you a cake.'

'Well, look at the positives,' Punk-Princess166 said. 'Too much sugar is bad for you.'

Arthur made a mental note not to trust Steve if he ever got lost in a tunnel. He didn't even have any sugar cane to leave as an asset in case he died; perhaps he could leave his red trainers instead, but that was pretty much all he had to offer.

Suddenly Arthur stopped walking; his sister bumped into Steve, knocking his torch and breaking it. They had been so busy talking that they hadn't noticed where they were.

'I think we've found something,' Arthur said. 'And it might just be our way out of here.'

In front of them was a large room with a high ceiling. It was lead grey, like most things around here, but there was something different about this space: a mining cart stood before them, resting on red tracks that led away from them down the tunnel. And there was definitely room in the cart for two humans and a mob.

For the first time since he'd set foot in the Overworld, Arthur felt lucky.

He moved closer and read the sign on the back of the cart.

TRAIN: 01

DESTINATION: TEMPLE

'Cowabunga!' exclaimed Punk-Princess166.

Arthur was right! The tracks would lead to an exit from these tunnels. It would take them straight to the temple, saving them time and allowing them to rest a little too. There was only one problem – and this really was a shame, because things had been going so well.

The room was packed with red-eyed zombies.

CHAPTER 14

ARTHUR OF THE DEAD

Zombies: dead, decaying, senseless creatures, with rotten teeth and brain-thirsty eyes. In the Overworld, they were green and blocky, with evil red eyes.

The zombies spotted Steve, Arthur and Punk-Princess166 straight away. Hundreds of red eyes turned as the zombies began moving towards them.

'You got a plan, Mallu?'

'Not dying?'

'Yeah, sounds good.'

'Let's do that then.'

Steve drew his sword and fixed his helmet on to his head. Punk-Princess166 and Arthur grabbed their swords and joined the warrior. They were only wooden swords, but they were better than no swords at all.

Arthur wished they could run away, back to the little house on the surface, but they were too exhausted – they would probably be caught by the hordes of zombies before they could get back there. All they could do now was get to the mining cart and use it to help them reach the temple. That was their best shot at getting closer to Herobrine's sword.

'We need to get in that cart,' Arthur said. 'It's the best chance we have.'

'I don't know whether you've noticed, but there are a lot of zombies in front of it,' his sister replied. 'And you really don't want to find out what they'd like to do to us.'

Arthur signalled to Steve and Punk-Princess166 that they should all keep moving towards the cart. The zombies moved forward too with their arms outstretched, reminding Arthur of the resurrected mummies from old Hollywood movies. They groaned as they slowly approached the group.

'Well, we'll have to get rid of them and clear

ourselves a path,' he said. 'Steve, how good are you with that sword?'

Steve smiled. 'I was the best mob around. I don't know if I've already mentioned this, but I was once an adventurer like you, until –'

'You were hit by an arrow in the knee,' Punk-Princess166 said. 'Yes, we've heard that story before.'

An idea suddenly occurred to Arthur. An idea that might just be clever enough to save them from these monsters. Without hesitating, he grabbed his torch and lifted the beam up high, shouting insults at the nasty green creatures approaching them.

'Hey, rotten avocados!' he shouted. 'I taste much better than those two! Over here! And I'm a limited-time promotion.'

The zombies turned on him with hungry eyes that followed his every move. Arthur headed towards the other side of the room, hoping the zombies would behave like a herd. That's what he'd learned from watching *The Walking Dead*, *Shaun of the Dead*, *Z Nation* and *Juan of the Dead*. Arthur crossed his fingers and hoped that the zombie TV shows and films had got it right.

'What are you doing, User?' Steve called.

'Saving our butts!' Arthur shouted. 'Just run to the cart – I'll follow you!'

He held the torch up as high as he could, shaking it from side to side and using his free hand to beat the wall with his wooden sword. Several of the zombies were drawn by the sound and the light. Punk-Princess166 had once said that the Overworld monsters were afraid of light, but as he only had one torch these monsters seemed to be intrigued rather than frightened.

'Run!' Arthur shouted.

'We're not leaving you behind,' his sister called.

'I'll be there soon – you need to get in the cart *right now*!'

Arthur continued distracting the zombies' attention while Punk-Princess166 and Steve dashed across the room and into the cart, finishing off a few zombies in their way. Arthur was right – the zombies followed one another without noticing what was really happening around them. Herd mentality – just as he'd suspected!

'Arthur, come on!' shouted his sister.

He could see the zombies' faces drawing nearer and nearer; he could smell their rotten stench and hear their groans. They were closer than he would have liked them to be. Far too close.

Arthur realized he was going to have to run *very* fast to get to the cart and avoid turning into zombie lunch. He grabbed the hilt of his sword and sprinted towards the cart. Some of the zombies were already horribly close, but he drove them back by striking them with the torch. Arthur was definitely not a skilled warrior, but his clumsy attacks seemed to help clear a path for him. He forced his way through, channelling all his fear and anger into striking at the zombies surrounding him.

Swearing under his breath, he saw Steve and Punk-Princess166's anxious faces as they waited in the cart for their last passenger.

Arthur ran faster, but suddenly his feet slipped on the smooth floor and he fell forward, banging his head. He felt a blast in his skull; blood gushed from his forehead. He tried to get up, but his foot ached so badly that he couldn't help screaming. It was one of the most painful things he'd ever experienced.

Some of the zombies were just three steps away, and their outstretched hands were almost close enough to grab him. Arthur shut his eyes, accepting the facts: he was going to be killed and turned into a zombie. He blurted out the kind of bad words that would have got him in a lot of trouble back home. Arthur could hear the zombies' feet shuffling across the smooth floor as they surrounded him. He felt a hand on his back; blocky fingers pulled at his shirt. *They've reached me*, he thought. *They've caught me.* He wished he'd been able to help his sister get back home. Instead he would die in that world, far away from his family and friends.

Surfacing from his self-pity, Arthur suddenly realized that it was taking longer than it should for him to be bitten.

He opened his eyes slowly, one at a time. He could just about see the monsters – they were attacking Steve, who now fought beside Arthur, wielding his sword with more skill than Arthur had ever seen before. The mob struck and struck; their enemies fell without a chance to strike back.

Steve helped the User to stand up; Arthur leaned

on his square shoulders to hop into the cart. He hadn't got there quite as quickly as he'd wanted to, but in the end he'd made it.

'Thank you so much, Steve,' he said, while Punk-Princess166 helped him up into the cart. 'You saved my life.'

The warrior smiled. 'I'm a warrior,' he said. 'This is my –'

Steve couldn't finish his sentence. Instead, he screamed in pain. Arthur looked down and saw the creature that had sunk its teeth into Steve's leg: a baby zombie, so small they hadn't spotted it, but it had small enough teeth to bite into the only part of the warrior's body that was not protected by his metal armour. The little monster clung to his victim's leg until Steve cut its head off with a quick blow. Arthur and Punk-Princess166 didn't know what to say; they sat, frozen, with their eyes wide.

'I don't think today is my lucky day,' the warrior said. 'Just carry on without me. You need to reach the temple.'

'You're our friend,' Arthur said. 'There's no way we're going to leave you behind.'

'We can help you heal,' said Punk-Princess166. 'All we need is a Potion of Weakness and a golden apple.'

Steve smiled. He seemed calm despite what had just happened to him, as if he had been programmed to deal with whatever life threw at him. He slew two more zombies that were approaching them, then began pushing the cart with his shoulders. It started to move.

'That's good of you to say, Users, but I'll be putting you at risk – and there's no time to waste,' he answered. 'This is it for me. I was bitten – the transformation will start soon. If you'd like to honour me, keep on fighting against the Red King and promise me that Herobrine will never be awakened. Save yourselves. And keep safe!'

'Steve, don't!' Arthur shouted. 'Get into the cart!'

Arthur and his sister kept shouting at Steve to jump in, but the cart was already speeding away down into the tunnel. As it gained momentum, jolting over the tracks, they looked back at the last image of Steve they would ever see. The warrior disappeared from view, engulfed in a crowd of green zombies.

CONCEPTS OF THE OVERWORLD

PART FIVE: Death

By Punk-Princess166

When I was just a player, sitting on a chair on the other side of the computer screen, I wasn't worried about death. In the end, pressing one button was all it took for me to appear again at my spawn point. One of the hardest things I learned about the Overworld is that there is no button you can press here to start again. People just die and never come back.

And that's it.

CHAPTER 15

THE OTHER SIDE OF DARKNESS

Loss strikes people in different ways. Some scream. Some weep. Some faint. But, for some people, there is nothing but silence; every sound is muffled.

That's how Arthur and Punk-Princess166 felt, huddled together as the cart ran along the track, driven by an invisible force. There was nothing they could do or say. Steve was dead, and they felt they were to blame – they'd dragged him into all this. Just as they'd dragged in all the Steves who'd died at the village. Their quest might well achieve nothing, and so many people had already died.

'We should've gone back,' Arthur said. He was close to tears. 'We could've jumped out of the cart and helped him.'

Punk-Princess166 shook her head. She was trying even harder than Arthur to stop herself from crying.

'There was nothing we could do for him back there, Arthur,' she said. 'He must have known that as soon as he'd been bitten. All we can do is carry on and do what we've got to do. Maybe when it's over we can come back here with the cure for him, but right now we've only got one option: to carry on.'

Arthur stared at the tunnel they were travelling through. Every now and again, the stones around them would twinkle. The only areas they could see properly were the ones where there were still torches fixed to the walls. This world was so confusing. Fire would just go on burning if you left it untouched; trees would remain standing even when their trunks had been cut down . . . There was no logic here.

His sister was probably right that this was the place where the Red King had set out with his ambitious plans – mining ores and creating his empire, block by block.

Through his sadness, Arthur couldn't help but be impressed. It must have taken the owner of these tunnels so long to build them.

'We'll find a way to save Steve eventually, Noobie,' said his sister. 'I'm sure of it. A Potion of Weakness and a golden apple. When we can get hold of those, we can come back and save Steve.'

'I hope so,' Arthur said.

They rolled on, the mining cart rattling on its tracks as they moved deeper into the darkness. Then the cart began to dip, descending so it could gain enough speed to go up the ascent ahead: a steep climb as high as a skyscraper. It was like being on the most dangerous rollercoaster ever invented.

'I'd love to figure out how this cart can run without an engine or anything,' Arthur said.

Punk-Princess166 explained to him that the person who had built all of this had used redstone, which can transmit power in the Overworld, and that his nickname – the Red King – had probably come from that too. As she spoke, the cart surged higher and higher. It jolted so hard that Arthur thought they would be knocked over the edge of the tracks. A chill rose in the pit of his stomach. He held his sister's hands tight and shut his eyes. Arthur definitely wasn't cut out to be a hero. He wasn't brave, he wasn't strong, and he lacked the sort of courage that Steve had. He was just a kid scared to death, caught in a world that seemed to be trying to kill him at every turn.

This was what Arthur was thinking when he saw a glimmer of light ahead of them. It steadily shaped itself into something he could recognize: a way out into the daylight!

Sparks flew off both sides of the track as the mining cart braked. Arthur held on tight, terrified that they would crash. But the cart came to a halt without anyone getting any more injuries. The two passengers jumped out as soon as they could.

'We're alive,' Arthur said, amazed. 'We're alive!'

'I'm as amazed as you are,' his sister said.

They kneeled and looked around them. *We better not speak too soon*, Arthur thought. *What if we've ended up trapped in a creepers' nest? If creepers even have nests* . . .

But luck was on their side. They had turned up in the middle of a dense forest; square trees surrounded them. There was plenty of greenery and lots of animals too – deer, birds, and even a bear roaming about in the distance, unfazed by the new arrivals. But the most interesting thing of all stood directly in front of them: a blue and green stone construction with columns. The temple they had been searching for. A red flag shimmered at its top, and it had a double wooden gate that was firmly shut. They could tell it was the right place – a bright glowing sign flashed on and off above the entrance.

THE PRIESTESS'S TEMPLE

I CAN READ YOUR FORTUNE. I CAN BRING

YOUR MISSING HUSBAND OR WIFE

BACK TO YOU IN THREE DAYS.

SPECIAL OFFER: BUY TEN CONSULTATIONS,

GET THE NEXT ONE FREE!

Arthur and Punk-Princess166 stared at each other and then looked back at the sign. The sign reminded Arthur of the fortune tellers in street stalls back in his home city. Surely this couldn't be a real priestess's temple?

But there wasn't much they could do – if they

really wanted help, they'd better keep an open mind and find out for themselves what was inside the building. Anything that would get them closer to finding Herobrine's sword and defeating the Red King would do.

'I guess we have to take a chance,' Punk-Princess166 said. 'Stay right behind me and run away at the first sight of danger.'

'I was already all set to do the last part.'

'Well, you're a boy. I have to spell everything out for you, just in case.'

They grabbed their wooden swords and approached slowly, looking everywhere for any traps or signs of danger. Their eyes were wide open and their ears strained to hear every tiny sound.

Arthur wished Steve was with them, with his large sword and his shining armour – everything would have been different then. Steve wouldn't have been afraid of this place, just like he hadn't been afraid of the enderman; he would have walked straight up to the temple door and knocked.

But Steve was dead. The brave warrior was now a zombie.

What chance do we have if anyone attacks us? Arthur wondered.

He saw his sister raise her hand to knock on the door, but before she could do so, the door opened wide and a figure appeared in the entrance.

'You've been out here a while, haven't you, Users?' asked the figure. 'I've been watching you cringing with fear for quite some time. Hi. My name's Alex, and I'd rather you didn't get yourselves killed by a bear on my doorstep. It wouldn't be good for business.'

Arthur stared at the figure before them. It was square and blocky like all the Steves, but this was the first female mob they had seen here. She had big green eyes, blonde hair, giant earrings, brightly coloured clothes and a golden tiara. The priestess turned to them and smiled.

CHAPTER 16

THE PRIESTESS AND MR LETTUCE

Arthur and Punk-Princess166 stared at the mob. She turned inside and gestured for them to follow her. Then she walked into the temple and out of sight. With no other option – and no time to think of a better plan – they hurried after her, making sure the door was closed behind them. Letting a bear kill them wasn't on either of their to-do lists.

'I was very surprised when I heard noises coming up from the mine,' Alex said. 'That place has been deserted for years.'

'Did you know it belongs to the Red King?' Arthur asked.

Alex shrugged her shoulders. 'Everyone knows that, kid. That was where I saw him for the first time, many years ago. He used to be a User like you; but he ceased to exist in your world a long time ago. I predicted from the start that he would be a problem for the Overworld. Now, come over here, I'm making some tea.'

Alex pointed out where the bathrooms were and showed them a room where they could rest if they wanted to. This place was her house, and all travellers were welcome, she said. The temple was large, decorated with plants and glazed tiles. The incense smelled strongly of cinnamon, making Arthur sneeze continually, the way strong perfume or even washing powder would at home. The cinnamon smell seemed to get everywhere.

'How long have you lived here for, Alex?' asked Punk-Princess166. 'Perhaps you can help us; we're looking for –'

'Herobrine's sword,' interrupted the priestess. 'That's the only way you'll be able to get back to your home on the other side.'

'How do you know that?' asked Arthur. 'We haven't said anything about it yet.'

Alex said nothing. She smiled slightly and led

them into a huge kitchen. There were endless cupboards, lots of pots and a giant sink, and everything was spotless. On a table were all kinds of cakes, loaves of bread, fruit, roast meats, glasses of juice and milk, and even a bowl of multicoloured salad. Just looking at it all made Arthur's stomach rumble – he hadn't eaten for hours and hours. Before Alex had even offered, Arthur sat down at the table and grabbed a slice of bread and a glass of orange juice. Food from the Overworld wasn't as tasty as food from the real world, but he was so hungry that right then the bread and juice tasted like the finest food he'd ever eaten.

'I thought you might be hungry,' said the priestess. 'Please, eat as much as you like. We've got a lot to talk about if you're still planning on going through with your mad idea of looking for Herobrine's sword.'

'Thank you very much for your hospitality,' said Punk-Princess166. 'We'll pay you back somehow, when we can.'

Arthur didn't waste any time saying thank you. He was too busy gobbling down as much food as he could. As he was vegetarian, he put the meat aside, but he was delighted with everything else. The priestess fetched the tea that had been boiling on the stove and joined them, helping herself to a slice of cake.

As they were scoffing down the food, Arthur heard a sound behind him. It was like the hiss of a cobra, or even . . . a burning fuse. He would recognize that sound anywhere in the world: a creeper was about to blow up!

Had they been tricked? He could see then that green legs were approaching them with slow but firm steps. Arthur and his sister dived under the table, and Arthur shut his eyes tight and waited for the massive blast, ready to be thrown into the air.

Panic settled deep in his stomach . . . He could hear the burning fuse . . . That unwavering noise, and then . . .

Nothing happened.

Arthur opened his eyes slowly. The creeper was there, by the table, standing still as if he was waiting for an order.

'I can see you've met Mr Lettuce,' said the

priestess. 'And that you're as biased as everyone else in the Overworld.'

Arthur looked at his sister, but she seemed as lost as he was. He couldn't believe a creeper might not try to kill him. One of the main things he had learned in the Overworld was that creepers were bad.

'So you mean he won't blow himself up and kill me?' Arthur asked, still shivering.

Alex burst out laughing as though this was a hilarious joke.

'Children, Mr Lettuce is a gentleman! He's my butler,' she explained. 'We met when I was a little girl. Please, get out from underneath the table and behave like normal people. Your food will go cold.'

They came out from under the table, still worried that the creeper might blow up any minute. They sat in their seats again and stared as the monster carried the dirty dishes to the sink. Arthur and Punk-Princess166 watched the creeper wash every plate carefully and place it on the draining-board to dry.

'The biggest mistake people make is believing that everyone is the same,' said Alex. 'Believing that all creepers are bad, and that all Steves are good.

Following that logic, since the Red King is bad, all other Users must be bad too. Children, it is always foolish to be biased.'

Arthur felt a little guilty for not believing in the priestess when they'd first arrived. He had judged too quickly, just like so many adults did back home – deciding whether a person was good or bad on the basis of how they looked. Arthur apologized to the priestess and the creeper, but Alex waved away his apology.

'You weren't to know,' she said. 'Let's forget about it. We need to talk about what brought you here. I'm a fortune teller, so I can see parts of the future and parts of the past too, but I can't always see the whole picture. I need to know everything from the start. How did you end up in the Overworld? And how did you find my house?'

Arthur and his sister nodded. They would do anything to try and make sense of all the craziness they were caught up in. They had travelled for far too long from place to place, as if carried by the wind. If there was a chance of finding some real answers, then they'd take it, whatever it was.

Punk-Princess166 began telling their story, from the floppy disc in the kitchen drawer to the numbers flashing on the computer screen and all that followed. She told Alex about what had happened in the forest, the people in the village, the Red King's attack, the telephone booth and the warrior who had given up his life to protect theirs, hoping they would find a way to defeat the enemy and bring peace to the Overworld again. And then, as she spoke of the friend she had lost, Arthur's sister finally let herself weep.

CHAPTER 17

THE PROPHECY

Alex listened as the siblings told their story. She didn't interrupt them; in fact she barely moved, just sipping her black tea every so often. When Punk-Princess166 finally came to that part where they had found the priestess, she nodded.

'Everything has happened just as I foresaw it would,' she said, in a tone of voice that made it clear that that wasn't good news. 'Herobrine knows he has a chance to get back to the Overworld now. He's dead, but he dreams about returning. And the dreams of the dead are very dangerous things, children.'

Arthur sat up as Mr Lettuce took away his dirty juice glass and empty plate. There was something on his mind. 'Do you mean Herobrine is aware of everything going on here?' he asked. 'That everything that's happening is exactly what he wants to happen?'

The priestess nodded. 'It's the only thing we can be sure about,' she said. 'Perhaps even the Red King doesn't realize it, but he is just a pawn in Herobrine's complex game. You cannot think of Herobrine as a person or a mob – he's different. Ancient. Herobrine existed before your world and ours; he transformed himself, travelling across many universes and taking them over one by one. He is worshipped as a god in other worlds. He is a creature of madness and chaos.'

'How do you know all this?' Arthur asked.

Alex didn't answer. She just walked out of the kitchen, leaving them alone.

'Do you really think it's true?' Arthur asked. 'That we're all doing exactly what Herobrine wants?'

'I don't know what to believe now,' Alex called back to him from outside the kitchen door. 'Things are a lot more complex than I had previously thought.'

When the priestess walked back into the room,

she held a red book in her hands. She sat down and opened the book at a page in the centre, turning it so they could see it too. There on the page was a picture of a mob sat on a stone in the middle of the sea; he looked almost exactly like a Steve, but his eyes were shining white and he wore a wicked expression. A caption on the drawing read: *Herobrine – death that walks among us.*

So this was the infamous Herobrine, whose name inspired such fear in everybody. Alex took another sip of tea.

'Allow me to introduce you to the enemy of every universe,' she said. 'He's waiting for the right moment to return. You can guarantee that he already knows both of you, and he knows your quest too. There's a reason why that sword is so powerful. According to the prophecy in this book, it is the only thing capable of cutting the boundaries between different worlds, thus setting Herobrine free from the Nether . . . and opening the gaps between universes.'

The priestess turned a few pages and read out part of some kind of poem.

The hand he hates most will open the door;
Herobrine shall return, claiming yet more.
Through the hands of the Users, destruction
shall come,
As to power's corruption these Users
succumb.

'In other words, the guy who wrote this book thinks we'll set Herobrine free,' said PunkPrincess166. 'He thinks we're going to find that monster and let him loose to destroy everything there is? And, even worse than that, he says we'll be corrupted!'

Alex shook her head. 'Believe me, kids, prophecies are always problematic,' she said. 'The more you try to run away from them, the faster they come true. And this prophecy says that a User will set Herobrine free. No one knows when or how, but a User *will* be the one to bring that evil back to the Overworld.'

Arthur rose and paced around the kitchen. He didn't want to believe a single thing he'd just heard, and if he could've, he would've run out of that temple and not looked back. Apart from the chance to eat some food, nothing good had come of their visit. 'We travelled all the way here because we were told you could help us find the sword, Alex,' he said. 'We've got to keep looking for it – we need to get back home. Steve is dead because of this mission; his village was destroyed because of it.'

Mr Lettuce placed a tray full of pastries on the table and then walked away, before putting on his apron and beginning to do the dishes. The three of them watched him for a while.

'No one has said you should stop searching,' said the priestess, straightening up. Her tone was serious. 'The only thing I've said is that your path and Herobrine's will cross. My mother was killed because of the sword prophecy too. The Red King has also been looking for the sword for years, and my mother was the only person who knew where it was. I was still a child when the Red King took her away and kept her locked up, searching for an answer to his question until her death. He never knew that she had left the book behind, and that I, the child he had abandoned to die alone, would one day become a greater priestess than my mother ever was.'

The siblings sat in silence as they absorbed Alex's words.

'So what do you think we should do?' asked Punk-Princess166. 'We have to do everything we can to stop Herobrine returning to this world – or going to ours.'

'You must keep on doing what you've been doing,' the priestess answered. 'Keep on fighting against the Red King and searching for the sword. But you must think carefully about every step you take. You will be tempted; the enemy will resort to anything to make sure that the prophecy is fulfilled. The future can change, and not all prophecies come true, but you must fight hard to avoid your fate.'

Arthur stared out of the window at the shining sun that held back all those monsters that ruled the night here. He could make out the remains of the creatures that had been destroyed by the daylight when it came, reminding him of the monsters that would return after nightfall. Perhaps the Overworld wasn't so different from other worlds, including his: monsters emerging at night, ready to catch whatever they can, bent on destroying everything and bringing evil. Hostile mobs and cruel humans weren't so different, after all.

'So how are we going to find the sword, then?' asked Punk-Princess166. 'If all our options lead us to Herobrine, I think we might as well go there and kick his butt as well as that stuck-up Red King's.'

'Ideally, I'd like to find an option where we don't end up meeting the lord of darkness, and getting our heads stuck on stakes,' concluded Arthur. 'I'm too young to bring an apocalypse to both the real world and the digital one.'

Mr Lettuce was standing close to his boss, staring; the Users felt just a tiny bit creeped out. Suddenly Alex smiled, her expression returning to normal. She flipped further ahead through the book.

'I think the time has come to talk about more interesting things. I hope you're ready, Users. It's not a coincidence that the sword has remained hidden for so long.'

Arthur couldn't think past all the suffering that sword had caused. He sat still and listened to what the priestess had to say. It couldn't be worse than what they'd already heard, could it?

CHAPTER 18

NICE TO MEET YOU, AMELIA

They listened attentively while Alex explained what had happened to the Diamond Sword at the end of the war against Herobrine, when the First Users had departed. Apparently several mobs had come up with a plan to keep the world safe. Attempts had been made to destroy the sword, but no substance was strong enough to do so. The wise elders, including Old Steve, got together to decide where the sword should be kept. They came up with several suggestions for places to hide it: at the base of a waterfall, inside the belly of an ender dragon, in a box in the sky, or even under Ms Estrela's mattress (apparently her bakery made such bad cakes that nobody ever went to her place, which made it ideal). But in the end it was decided that Hattori Hanzō, the most honourable swordsman to fight in the war, would guard the sword and keep away anyone who tried to find it.

'And how are we meant to find this Hattori Hanzō?' asked Arthur. 'If I was in charge of looking after a weapon of mass destruction, I would hide in a cave and never come out.'

'Noobie has a point,' said Punk-Princess166.

'Hattori doesn't live in a cave,' Alex told them. 'At least, he didn't when I last visited him. Hanzō is a private person, but he's not as unapproachable as the legends might make you think. His home is far away from here, in an ice biome on the other side of the forest.'

'Houston, we have a problem,' Punk-Princess166 murmured.

Arthur couldn't help feeling disheartened. He didn't have a clue how to cross an entire forest and reach an ice biome alive. They had already wasted hours travelling through the woods and the mine, and, more importantly, they'd lost a friend to the zombies in the process. How on earth would they find Hattori Hanzō?

'Don't worry about it,' Alex said, as though she could read his thoughts. 'I know someone who can help you. I have a friend who can take you there. She is the only person left in the whole region who still has redstone – she'll have enough to make the journey. Obviously she'll need payment, but I'm sure we can sort it all out.'

As Alex walked off, the siblings couldn't help looking panicked – none of that would be any good to them. The truth was that they didn't have any money or precious stones or anything. All they had were their wooden swords and the donations given to them at Steve's village: basic equipment and a few packs of pixelated food. As far as they were concerned, none of that would be valuable enough to trade with.

'We haven't got anything,' Arthur said. 'We're totally broke. I never imagined that we'd need money to save the world.'

'Playing Batman is easy,' his sister remarked. 'The hard part is being Bruce Wayne. I heard that in a podcast a while ago and it sounded appropriate for wannabe heroes.'

'Spider-Man is poor,' Arthur pointed out.

'That's why he's the superhero who gets beaten the most. Believe me, if he had the money to get a high-tech suit of armour or a Batmobile, he would. We're the same. We should have collected some valuable stuff along the way – any ores would have helped.'

Arthur put his hands in his pockets and paced up and down the room. Mr Lettuce seemed to be watching him, as though he was trying to work out why Arthur looked so anxious. Nothing had changed when Alex came back into the room sporting a straw hat and holding a bag in her hands. The priestess gestured for the Users to follow her and asked her butler to start getting dinner ready, as she hoped to return before nightfall.

'I won't be long, Mr Lettuce,' she said. 'Please have it all sorted and don't forget to cook my favourite soup. Thanks ever so much.'

The creeper made the burning fuse noise, which seemed to be a signal that he had understood Alex's orders. The two kids rose and followed the priestess as she ambled along the hallways towards the temple's exit. She had mentioned that there was a village nearby, and that the woman who was going to help them lived there.

'Alex, we have a problem,' said Punk-Princess166. 'We're totally broke.'

'That's not a problem at all,' the priestess replied as she walked. She hardly even seemed to be paying attention.

They walked into the forest behind the temple and found a path. Alex said there had once been a city in the area but it had been destroyed by the Red King in his search for rare redstone he could use to keep all the machines in City 01 running. He used those powerful stones to begin his iron and black smoke expansion, changing the Overworld so profoundly that even the texture of the wood blocks was altered, not even caring about the mobs who lost their family and friends because of him. Everything he did was 'in the name of progress' – that was what he used to say as he ordered creepers to destroy entire forests.

'Why did he do that?' asked Arthur. 'What did he

gain by destroying it all? Or by killing mobs?'

The priestess scratched her head thoughtfully. 'Some people don't need a reason to destroy things,' she replied at last. 'I lost my mother because of him, and I have never found out why. I've come to the conclusion that mad people don't need a reason to do bad things. It's just in their blood.'

Five minutes later they reached the village. It was smaller than Steve's village. Some wooden houses stood around the main square, which had one small stone bench under a tree. Some mobs were going about their business: farmers, smiths, salesmen, and even a young girl playing the accordion.

'There she is!' said Alex, sounding thrilled. 'Exactly where I thought she'd be. Please, come on over.'

Arthur looked in the direction the priestess was pointing, towards a table with several people around it. He quickly realized what all the fuss was about: there was an arm-wrestling contest going on, and male mobs were queuing up to face a young female mob. She was tall with strong arms, and she was made up of brown pixels. She wore a black jacket, aviator goggles on her head, and tall boots that would leave any victim she kicked covered in bruises. A woodcutter had just lost an arm wrestle with her; she laughed out loud as he added precious stones to her pile of winnings.

Alex reached out to hold Arthur and Punk-Princess166's hands as they inched through the small crowd until they faced the young woman in the centre. Everyone turned to stare at the new arrivals, especially the Users – to the mobs they were strange-looking creatures made of flesh who'd only ever existed in the Overworld's mythical past. Arthur felt like an animal in a zoo under the scrutiny of all those eyes.

'Hey, Amelia,' the priestess said. 'Have you got time to help a friend save the world? I swear I'll pay you this time.'

The gambler finished beating her latest rival, then looked at her friend with a wry smile. 'If I had a gem for every time you've promised to pay me, I'd be richer than the Red King,' she answered. 'I see you've brought some friends – this is going to be interesting . . .'

'I promise it will be the best adventure you've ever had,' replied the priestess. 'Monsters, risk-taking . . . and two children even more lost than we were when we were teenagers.'

Arthur felt a bit apprehensive looking at the woman – she seemed like the kind of person who would set a house on fire just for the fun of it. But he knew this wasn't the time for being choosy, especially as they didn't have any money of their own to pay for help. They had no other options. Arthur exchanged a glance with his sister and hoped they weren't getting themselves into an even bigger mess.

'Nice to meet you, Users,' the arm-wrestler said. 'My name is Amelia and I am the best mercenary the Overworld has ever known.'

CONCEPTS OF THE OVERWORLD

PART SIX: Mercenaries

By Punk-Princess166

In the Overworld, like in our own world, there are all kinds of jobs. You can get anything you want, as long as you have the right amount of ore to trade. And of all of the people with jobs in the Overworld, the mercenaries are at the top. They will do any job for anyone, and they can be paid in gold, rubies or whatever they like best.

Not all mercenaries become notorious for being amoral, unscrupulous thieves and liars, but most of them would admit that anyone doing business with mercenaries is taking a risk.

CHAPTER 19

SERVICE CONTRACT

Amelia grabbed all the winnings she had earned wrestling against her rivals. Then she walked to the centre of the village with Alex and the siblings, where they sat down together under the tree. Alex began to tell Amelia everything that had happened so far, explaining how the Users had come to her temple and where they were hoping to go next. She stressed how important everything was, and told Amelia how terrible the consequences would be if the mission failed.

'So you mean these two are our best hope of salvation?' asked Amelia, laughing out loud. 'The only ones who can defeat the Red King and stop Herobrine from returning?'

However annoying it was to hear Amelia sounding so incredulous, Arthur had to agree with her. He really couldn't see how he and his sister would be able to do anything about all this – a few days ago they had been arguing about who would do the dishes. But he knew his sister felt differently.

'My name is Punk-Princess166,' she said, crossing her arms, 'and this is my brother, Arthur, or Noobie Saibot. We've survived an enderman's attack and a cave filled with zombies. I think we're ready for anything, whether it's here or at the end of the world. All we need is for you to lead us to Hattori Hanzō. After that, we will find our own way.'

Amelia looked at Punk-Princess166 with a different expression then, as though perhaps she was worthy of her attention after all. 'So, this one's an angry one!' she said. 'Well, I have a hot-air balloon which could take you there. I've already done this journey once before with the priestess, but I should warn you, it won't be cheap.'

That was just the comment that Arthur had been dreading – because they couldn't pay her anything. And, judging by the large sums she made arm wrestling, they would need a lot of money to pay for Amelia's help. It was no good trying to lie or strike a deal.

'We haven't got any money,' Arthur said. 'Nothing. Not even a precious stone, if that's your currency here.' He tried to come across as serious and straightforward. 'We've only made it this far because we've had help from people, and some of those people paid with their lives. The only thing we can offer is the promise that we will do all we can to make sure that neither Herobrine nor the Red King destroys the world.'

'Well, all that just means you can't pay me, doesn't it?' Amelia said.

'Yeah, pretty much,' said Punk-Princess166. 'So are you going to help us or not?'

Amelia shrugged her shoulders. 'How about this: I'll go with you until you find something that can pay off the debt.' She grabbed a small wooden stick and started drawing calculations on the ground as she worked out the costs. 'Two diamonds and a ruby. I heard the Red King has a large stock of ores in City 01. I'll give you a lift in exchange for some of those. Would that work for you?'

Punk-Princess166 stretched out her hand ready for shaking, a gesture that meant the same thing in all worlds: an agreement had been reached. Arthur was pleased to have someone else joining them on their quest. Without Steve they didn't have anyone adventurous on their side, and, above all, they needed someone with a strong survival instinct. Amelia wasn't as selfless as Steve the warrior had been, but they couldn't complain. They were getting a lift out of there.

'When can we set out?' asked Punk-Princess166. 'We're in a bit of a hurry.'

'I'll need an hour to get the balloon ready but then we'll be on our way as fast as we can go,' replied the adventurer. 'Alex knows where I live – meet me there. We'll set out as soon as everything's prepared.'

Arthur and his sister shook hands with Amelia, and then she left to get everything ready.

'There is only one person who can take you to Hattori Hanzō, and that person is Amelia,' Alex told them. 'But still, I need to give you some advice.

I can see a terrible storm is approaching. It might sound like a cliché, but it's true. Some pieces are moving on the chessboard, but they are not yet clear for me to see – all I can say is that you must be careful. Both the Red King and Herobrine are watching every step that you take.'

Arthur watched the villagers going about their business, oblivious to the Users' presence, and to the fact that their fate was being discussed. They had no idea that two children were in charge of saving the world from total destruction. Arthur wished they had never slotted that floppy disc into the computer. If he hadn't been trying so hard to get his sister in trouble, things would probably be very different right now.

'Do you think we can actually beat them?' asked Punk-Princess166. 'The Red King has an army and Herobrine is the wickedest creature that has ever existed. I mean . . . *how* are we going to beat them?'

Alex burst out laughing. 'You still don't get it, do you? *They're afraid of you.* Herobrine has been defeated by Users once before, and the Red King is just a spoiled child. They are both afraid that you'll use the sword to defeat them once and for all. That's why the Red King offered you a chance to leave the Overworld in exchange for the sword. He would prefer to get you away from here, even if it meant letting you live, rather than take a chance against you in open battle.'

Arthur saw things clearly for the first time. The Red King must have thought it was safer to offer them an escape from that world instead of sending his creepers, zombies and endermen to destroy them for him – he'd had plenty of opportunities when he could have done that. Perhaps it was no coincidence that even though Steve's village was destroyed, he and his sister had survived – as if the enderman had been given clear orders not to hurt them. Perhaps the king was afraid. Maybe he wanted them to find the sword and leave, so that they would be out of his sight and no threat to him.

'But why hasn't he found Hattori?' asked Punk-Princess166. 'He seems to have all the resources he'd need to do it.'

'He's got all the resources, but they don't solve all the problems. Since ancient times, only two people have known the whereabouts of the Diamond Sword: my mother and Hattori Hanzō. When the Red King invaded the temple and took my mother away, leaving me behind because he thought I was too young to be any use to him, he was blind to the fact that I might know something. So I am the only person in the world apart from you and now Amelia who knows about Hattori and the hidden sword.'

Arthur nodded. He wanted to find out more, but it was time to meet back up with Amelia.

They rose and began walking; the priestess led them down a blue bricked path until they reached a stone house at the end of a thicket. They could see Amelia's balloon from there, ready and waiting, far off behind the trees. It was huge – there was room for about ten people inside its basket. It was the colour of sand and had a red square face painted on one of its sides. Giant letters spelled its name: the *Flying Baron*.

They approached; Amelia was seeing to all the final details, checking the sandbags, making sure the balloon had no punctures, and getting some food on board.

'About time,' she said when they arrived. 'I was about to go and find you.'

'We're five minutes early!' said Punk-Princess166.

'Well, I'm a very punctual person,' Amelia said.

Arthur and his sister left their belongings in the balloon basket and went to say goodbye to Alex. They were incredibly grateful to have found her when they did – just when all had seemed lost. The priestess gave them both a hug and told them to be careful. They would have to overcome many hurdles on the way if they were going to survive.

'And remember,' she said, 'Herobrine and the Red King are more scared of you than you are of them.'

Amelia gestured for them to head back to the balloon. She was keen to take off before nightfall – she didn't want any monsters attacking her beautiful *Flying Baron*. She began readying the balloon for take-off and asked them to get into the basket. 'Can we skip the goodbyes and get on with it before I get all emotional?' she said. 'You can always send her a postcard later, kids.'

Alex smiled. 'You're such a killjoy, Amelia.'

'The best killjoy ever,' Amelia replied.

They exchanged a last few words of good luck and advice about what they might face. Eventually, when they'd said goodbye, the balloon ascended into the sky, leaving the ground behind. At first it rose slowly. Then it powered on and gained speed, turning Alex and the village into tiny meaningless dots beneath them.

CHAPTER 20

HEAVIER THAN THE SKY

Arthur had never liked travelling by air. For him, flying was pretty much the worst thing in the world, especially take-off and landing, as statistically that's when most crashes happen. Nobody had thought to mention to Arthur that hot-air balloons are much more dangerous.

The basket swayed back and forth in the breeze like a ship in the ocean, and the strong wind on Arthur's face drew attention to all the dangers he might not have noticed from behind the little oval window of an aeroplane. High up in the Overworld sky, Arthur shivered all over.

'Is this your first time in a balloon?' asked Amelia, noticing his airsick expression. 'Don't worry, you'll get used to it. The *Flying Baron* is the safest method of transportation in the Overworld – a masterpiece when it comes to stability.'

'He'll never get used to it,' said Punk-Princess166. 'Our parents have taken us on plane trips loads of times, and he's always sick.'

Arthur tried to tell himself it would be all right, as that seemed like a better option than being scared to death. He looked ahead of him at the machine with redstone in its centre, which was generating all the heat needed to keep the balloon in the air. He still thought it was amazing that redstone was capable of generating renewable and almost-everlasting energy. No wonder the Red King had taken his name from redstone, and done all he could to get hold of more of it. Redstone was the driving force of the Red King's empire, enabling the mods, as his sister called them, that were behind every new creation, from telephone booths in the middle of nowhere to the incredible City 01.

It was getting dark, reminding Arthur that monsters were about to emerge down on the ground, ready to attack villages and anyone foolish enough to venture out of their home. But high in the sky it was calmer, as if nothing could reach them up there – no fear, no danger. Arthur decided the sensation of safety outweighed the discomfort he felt from flying and being so high up.

The balloon rocketed up through the air, and while his sister and Amelia chatted about their adventures, tiredness overtook Arthur and his eyes began to close. Slowly his thoughts began to drift away.

Fire . . .

Everywhere.

As the heat rose, Arthur tried desperately to work out where he was. Had the balloon caught fire? Had they fallen? Looking around, he couldn't tell what had happened – he was on the ground and there was no trace of the *Flying Baron*, Amelia or his sister. He was in a place that seemed to be made from blocks of redstone; rivers of lava flowed all around him. There were noises too, demonic screams and moans.

He began to walk around aimlessly – he needed

to find someone, anyone. This place looked a little like the Overworld, but it was very different. The only colours here were red and black; it was a vast, devastated land where nothing seemed to grow. It looked like any plant would die before its seed could produce even a sapling.

Arthur paced around and thought about calling out to his sister, but then he spotted an enderman and dashed to hide behind a stone. The last thing he needed was to catch that creature's eye. The monster disappeared in a purple cloud, and Arthur took a deep breath. Fear was taking over his mind and dread was suffocating him; it felt like someone was choking him to death.

Once the coast was clear, Arthur started walking again, searching for an exit. He tried to remember how he had ended up there. The last thing he could recall was being in the balloon, and . . .

Yes!

He was asleep! This was all a dream. None of this was real. It was just a nightmare he would wake up from in a few minutes. He tried to calm down. After all, he had been through a lot of stress in the past few days – this dream was probably just a consequence of the trauma he had undergone in the Overworld. He was in one of those rare dreams in which he had some awareness of where he was and could influence the dream around him however he wanted.

Arthur still had to try to be brave – an encounter with an enderman was never pleasant, even in a dream. He wiped the sweat off his forehead with the back of his hand as he reached a blind alley with a heap of stones at its end. The heap wasn't too big, so he thought he would be able to climb on top of it and gain a panoramic view of the area.

Arthur found his grip on the stones and began climbing. It wasn't hard – he reached the top in less than a minute. When he got there, he froze in shock. There, with his back towards him, he saw a Steve – perhaps his friend Steve. He wasn't wearing armour and he was gazing at something far away. Seeing Steve confirmed Arthur's suspicion that he was dreaming. He must have wanted to see his friend again – the friend he lost in such awful circumstances.

'Steve? Steve?' he asked, thrilled to see him. 'I've missed you!'

The figure began to turn.

'Steve?' it said. 'No. Herobrine. Welcome to the Nether, young Arthur.'

For the first time, Arthur saw the figure clearly. He was exactly like any Steve – same clothes, same face, even the same goatee. But one thing was different. Just like the picture in Alex's red book, Herobrine's eyes were completely white and they shone like endlessly burning suns.

'It can't be,' Arthur murmured. He shut his eyes tight. 'This is a dream. This is just a nightmare.'

'Of course it's a dream, you fool,' Herobrine said. 'But that doesn't mean it isn't real – or that your suffering won't be real.'

As soon as Herobrine finished speaking, a terrible headache hit Arthur, like someone was kicking him in the temple. He screamed out at the top of his lungs, falling to the ground and holding his head. The pain was unbearable. It seized his whole body until there was nothing else left; it was like an invisible hand was squeezing his brain until everything else vanished.

'My strength is increasing every moment,' said

Herobrine, in a voice barely louder than a murmur. 'It's just a matter of time before I will be strong enough to return to the Overworld and claim what's mine: each and every soul.'

Arthur reached out to grab on to a rock and pulled himself to his feet again. 'That will not happen,' he said. 'We won't allow it. I know the truth, Herobrine. You're scared of us – you're afraid that Users will once again prevent you from carrying out your diabolical schemes. You're just like any other dictator – a total idiot.'

Herobrine's eyes shone intensely, as if fuelled by his hatred for Arthur. 'A worm should know when to shut up,' he said. 'A worm should know how to behave.'

'So why haven't you learned, then?'

Before Arthur could even blink, Herobrine was standing beside him. Arthur could see every detail of his face and those eyes that shone so relentlessly.

Herobrine drew even closer to him, and said, 'In the Nether, Herobrine the dead awaits and dreams.'

He flicked his hand. Arthur flew high into the air, off the edge of the pile of stones and into an abyss, falling and falling and falling. His screams gradually died out, and Herobrine's face was the last thing he saw before –

He awoke and sat upright, startled and disorientated. His body was covered in sweat and his clothes were scorched all over; a stench of burning clogged his nose.

He looked around and saw his sister sleeping in a corner of the balloon basket. Amelia was busy piloting the balloon, whistling a song as she did so. The dream came flooding back to him. Without any warning, Arthur leaned over the edge of the basket and vomited everything in his stomach down over the Overworld.

CONCEPTS OF THE OVERWORLD

PART SEVEN: The Nether

By Punk-Princess166

General info: bad place.

Contents: fire, Herobrine, monsters, zombie pigmen. Everyone in the Nether wants to have your soul for breakfast. (Have I already told you about the zombie pigmen?)

Recommendation: run away, and never come back.

CHAPTER 21

STRATEGIC PAUSE

Dawn was fast approaching; the square sun would rise soon, as it always did. After he stopped being sick, Arthur woke his sister up and called Amelia over to tell them about his dream. He could still feel the Nether's heat on his face and Herobrine's voice buzzing in his head. He spared no detail – he told them about all the dream's horrors, and as he spoke his heart was filled with dread.

'So you had a dream about Herobrine,' said his sister, not convinced. 'It could have just been a dream.'

Arthur shook his head. 'No,' he said. 'Look at my shirt – a dream wouldn't do that. I was in the Nether. I *saw* Herobrine.'

They stared at him, baffled, and for a while nobody spoke. What hope did they have if Herobrine was already strong enough to manipulate telephone boxes and roam through a stranger's mind, even when he was imprisoned in the far reaches of the Nether? It was harder than ever to believe what Alex had said – that Herobrine was scared of Users. Arthur didn't think he had felt the full extent of his own fear until the moment he met Herobrine; now he was paralysed with dread.

'I think he just wants to scare you,' said Amelia. 'That's what bullies do: they push you and pull your hair, but it's mainly just to show you who's boss. If he wasn't afraid of you, he wouldn't have done that.'

'Do you really think he just wanted to scare us?' asked Punk-Princess166. 'That he just put on that whole performance to try to make us give up the fight against him?'

'He didn't seem that scared when he threw me into an abyss and made my head pretty much explode with pain.'

Amelia laughed out loud. 'But you're alive and back here without a scratch on you,' she said. 'It doesn't matter how big the villain is – at the end of the day, they're all like little kids. They're gross and they spit, but they're just wimps who don't have what it takes to survive a real fight.'

Amelia rose and went back to taking care of the balloon; every now and again she needed to adjust the route and check their speed. She told the siblings that soon they'd stop by a lake so that they could wash and rest before continuing their journey.

Arthur looked down at the vast stretch of forest they had left behind. A long river flowed through the countryside. Further ahead, about ten kilometres away, was the lake Amelia had mentioned – one of the largest Arthur had ever seen. There was nothing near it, not even a house, making it the ideal place to rest for a while.

'I'd love to have a bath,' murmured Punk-Princess166. 'I feel like a couple of skunks are going to crawl out of my armpits any minute.'

Arthur laughed. 'I thought you always smelled

this bad,' he said. He wouldn't have wasted that chance to tease his sister, even if Herobrine had been there in the balloon basket with them.

'No, the stink only hangs around when I spend time with you. Believe me, brother, if I could, I would keep away from your ugly face for a whole year. This has officially been the worst holiday ever.'

'Indeed.'

'That's exactly what I'm talking about – what kind of person says "indeed"? You're *such* a disappointment.'

The *Flying Baron* began descending, the air beating against the balloon as it flew. Arthur held on tight to the edge of the basket and shut his eyes; his fear of flying was taking over again. He glanced over at his sister – she seemed to be enjoying herself, a wicked smile on her face. Mallu had always been like this – she was the one with a spirit of adventure in their family, a trait she had inherited from their mum. Arthur was more like their dad, who was quiet and avoided taking unnecessary risks. He would never drive a car at fifty miles an hour if forty would do.

'Crew, we're ready for landing!' shouted Amelia. 'Welcome to Wind Lake.'

The balloon's basket hit the ground with such force that the passengers were flung about like rag dolls, but their pilot stayed standing, as though that always happened.

'You didn't say it would throw us around so much,' Arthur complained.

'What can I say?' replied Amelia, jumping out of the basket. 'I like surprises. Think of it as a bonus.'

They climbed out and stretched a bit, then filled some bottles with water and washed their faces. After that they took turns so that each of them could have a quick bath while the others got everything ready in preparation for continuing their journey.

Arthur sat facing the lake and wished they could stay there forever, feeling the gentle wind and splashing in the warm water, but he knew it wouldn't work out like that. They had to carry on searching, and they would have to deal with every hurdle they came across on their way. He thought about how things might be back home, and how his parents and his friends would be feeling; he thought about all the time that had passed and whether there'd still be anything of home left when they returned. He missed everything: his bed, his mother moaning because he'd left his socks all over the place, going skating and even going to school.

'What are you thinking about, Noobie?' his sister asked, sitting down beside him.

'I'm thinking about home. Do you reckon Mum and Dad have noticed we're missing yet?'

Punk-Princess166 paused for a moment, gazing at the calm surface of the lake. 'I don't know. Time here seems to pass differently. You only stayed at home a few minutes more than me, but when you got here I had already been in the Overworld for hours. Perhaps just a few minutes have passed since we left, or maybe it's been a few hours. We don't know. I'm trying not to think about it too much – otherwise it'll drive me mad.'

'You're already mad.'

Punk-Princess166 nodded. 'OK, fine – otherwise it'll drive me *totally* mad.'

Arthur grabbed a stone and hurled it at the lake,

trying and failing to make it skip across the water. It sank into the depths. 'Aren't you terrified after everything that's been going on here?' he asked. 'It's crazy . . . I mean, the way we ended up here, and what we're doing now?'

'Of course I'm scared, you idiot,' she answered. 'But I can't afford to let that fear paralyse me – the only solution is to use it to our advantage. I miss home, I feel like running away, but I can't do either of those things. I have to carry on.'

Arthur smiled. 'When did you get so mature, Mallu?'

'I guess it happened when you weren't looking.'

'We should talk like this more often.'

Punk-Princess166 tilted her head to the side. 'I don't think so,' she said. 'I'd get bored. Emotional talks are more your thing than mine.'

She patted her brother's arm and rose, walking towards the balloon where Amelia was getting everything ready for take-off. Arthur didn't know how to explain what had happened, but for the first time in a long time he felt at peace, as if a heavy weight had been lifted from his shoulders

for a moment. And in that moment, there was no
Red King and there was no Herobrine – there
was just a peaceful feeling of being at one with
nature; of knowing he was part of something
ancient and nameless.

CHAPTER 22

THE WINTER ON THE OTHER SIDE

They were airborne again, travelling fast along the horizon. According to Amelia, in a few minutes they would see the Stretch of Ice, the ice biome that was home to Hattori Hanzō, the guardian of Herobrine's sword. They were leaving the fields behind; green areas were becoming more and more scarce. A great expanse of whiteness rose up ahead of them, reflecting the sunlight.

Arthur and Punk-Princess166 were thrilled to be getting close; they looked over the edge of the balloon basket, watching the ground below turn from green to white almost in an instant. They were getting close to solving this whole mess and finding their way back home.

'Ladies and gentleman, boys and girls,' said Amelia. 'We are now in the White Lands of the Overworld, home to snowballs!'

This was the first time Arthur and Punk-Princess166 had ever seen so much snow and ice, and for a while they forgot they were in the digital world and that the snow there wasn't the same as it was where they came from.

The cold caught Arthur by surprise. The temperature dropped very suddenly from mild to below freezing. Arthur wished he'd been better prepared, but there was nothing he could do now, except hope he wouldn't die of hypothermia.

'The tip of my nose is frozen,' said Punk-Princess166. 'As in, I think it's actually frozen. I can barely feel it.'

'I think I can help,' their pilot said. 'I'm always ready for an emergency like this.'

She opened a suitcase and took out some huge overcoats with fluffy hoods. The siblings quickly put on their coats and they soon felt the heat returning to their extremities. The coats were way too big for them – Amelia was taller than them, and a lot squarer – but they didn't care. At least now they weren't going to die from the cold.

'I'll add those to your bill,' Amelia said. 'We can come to an agreement later.'

'I would pay a lot of money for this coat right now,' said Arthur.

'Wait until you see the bill, young man,' Amelia replied. 'If I remember rightly, we're close to Hattori Hanzō's home – he lives in a cabin beyond that hill. I brought Alex here a few years ago. Soon we'll land and continue on foot – there isn't a good landing spot beyond a certain point here.'

'You haven't got a sleigh and some husky dogs hidden in your suitcase, have you?' asked Punk-Princess166, staring at the rugged terrain below them.

'Unfortunately not. But I'll bear that idea in mind for the next trip.'

Amelia stopped talking so that she could concentrate on finding a place to land. They were losing altitude and could now see the shadow of the balloon across the ground; they would land in minutes. The engine that powered the balloon was slowing down, and Amelia advised her passengers to hold on tight. They didn't need telling twice.

Within minutes the *Flying Baron* touched down, with all passengers alive and in one piece. The Users climbed out of the basket as Amelia began to anchor the balloon to the ground. She told them that she wasn't going to deflate it – the powerful redstone engine ensured that she didn't have to. She said she would prefer to stay with the balloon while the two of them went to talk to Hattori Hanzō.

'But you'd better be quick,' she said. 'I don't want to be on the ground when night falls. If you aren't back before dusk, I'll take off and then come back tomorrow to find out if you're still alive.'

Arthur nodded and fixed his jacket.

'We'll come straight back,' said Punk-Princess166. 'How do we get to Hattori's house?'

Amelia pointed towards a large hill about two kilometres away. She said there were still about six hours of daylight left – enough to find the swordsman and get back to their meeting point.

'You need to go straight ahead. Hattori's cabin is on the other side of the hill,' Amelia told them. 'He doesn't trust strangers, so you must tell him that Alex sent you. He has seen Users before, so that should help make things easier for you.'

There was no time to waste. They said goodbye to Amelia and set out, trudging along the freezing ground, the cold piercing through their shoes and socks and reaching for their toes. Their teeth chattered and they could hardly feel their fingers.

'Remember how I always wanted to see snow?' asked Punk-Princess166.

'Yeah, you used to say that to Mum all the time.'

'Well, I've changed my mind. Snow is stupid. Cold is stupid. I want the boiling hot summer weather we get back home.'

'Me too.'

They plodded along for over half an hour. The *Flying Baron* was soon out of sight. There was total silence, only interrupted occasionally by the lonely howl of a wolf. The possibility of becoming a wolf's meal made them speed up, holding each other's hands to avoid falling. The toughest bit was climbing up the hill; they gripped on to the frozen stones and blocks of ice, every step seeming to take minutes. A journey that would only take about fifteen minutes in good weather took an hour here – plus there was the added danger of body parts freezing and falling off.

'If I don't die here,' said Punk-Princess166, 'remind me when we get back to kill you for finding that floppy disc.'

'You were the one who wanted to find out what was on it,' Arthur pointed out.

'And you were the one who found it! It's your fault. I'm just nosy. Sisters are always nosy.'

When they finally reached the top, they could see the cabin Amelia had told them about. It was a large wooden building with a tall chimney, and through the windows they could see what looked like the glow from a fireplace. This last detail had them hurrying down the slope as fast as they could go.

They had to be careful – they might slip and roll all the way down the hill. But Arthur couldn't think about anything except warming up by the sweltering fire inside that cabin. Herobrine, the Red King and indeed everyone from the Overworld was forgotten as he pictured himself sitting in front of the fireplace.

'I think we could –'

Arthur didn't have a chance to finish his sentence. He was hit hard on the shoulder; the blow was so strong that it knocked him down. The same seemed to have happened to his sister – she was rolling over next to him and crying out for help. Arthur saw the world spin round over and over again until he came to a halt at the foot of the hill. The pain struck, and he let out a scream; every part of his body hurt.

He put his hands on his knees to try to stand up and look for his sister. Then he saw two legs right in front of him, dressed in large black boots. He looked up further and saw a mob standing before him. He wore a black jumpsuit, and was as square-looking as Steve, Alex and Amelia, but he had a long white beard. He pointed a sword at Arthur's face.

'Trespasser,' he said. 'Speak your name so that Hattori Hanzō shall know whose life he is ending.'

Arthur decided it was probably best not to answer.

CHAPTER 23

HATTORI HANZŌ

Arthur looked up at the mob in front of him. On the bright side, they had found Hattori Hanzō. But, on a less positive note, he seemed to want to kill them.

The swordsman stood with his weapon still pointed at Arthur's face, staring down at him with a gaze that could cut a person in half.

'We were sent here by Alex the priestess!' shouted Punk-Princess166. 'We're looking for Herobrine's sword.'

As soon as Punk-Princess166 spoke, the mob let his sword drop a little and looked across at her. He hadn't quite lowered his sword enough for Arthur to stop worrying about it, but it did seem that now they had a chance to explain what was happening, rather than being hacked to pieces immediately.

Arthur rose, grateful to the cold for having numbed the pain of his injuries. He could see his sister approaching with her hands up in a gesture of peace, her eyes fixed on the warrior like a snake-charmer trying to communicate with the world's most dangerous cobra. She took each step slowly, calculatedly, under the watchful eyes of the swordsman.

'So what's brought you here?' the mob said. 'I will know whether you're telling the truth or not. You look like Users, but the Red King has many tricks. No disguise spell can fool me.'

Arthur moved towards his sister. 'This isn't magic,' he said, his voice shaking. 'Honestly, we're Users and we fell into your world by mistake. All we want to do is defeat the Red King and get back home. If we could do it without awakening Herobrine and having him invade my dreams, that would be even better.'

The warrior stroked his beard and made a thoughtful sound. There was a long pause; Hattori looked like he was making up his mind as to whether he should finish off the intruders. Then, without speaking, he turned and walked away with his sword still in his hand, leaving the siblings standing there, bewildered.

'Are you staying there or coming with me?' the mob asked as he walked. 'It's too cold for me to have a chat with you new Users out here.'

Arthur and Punk-Princess166 stood still for a moment, trying to work out whether they should follow this crazy man who acted like a murderer. But then they thought about the windows and the fire they had seen through them, and immediately ran after him. They tripped over and fell a few times, but eventually they managed to get into the cabin, shutting out the cold of the ice biome behind them.

'Thank you very much for having us,' said Punk-Princess166. 'You're the last hope we've got of finding the Diamond Sword.'

The swordsman's house was extremely clean and tidy, as if he'd thought very carefully about where each object should go. There were plant pots, decorative swords, tables, chairs, several shelves stacked with books, and an enormous fireplace filling the room with waves of heat. Arthur and his sister stood right in front of the flames, trying to dry themselves and their soaking-wet clothes.

'So you're the new Users,' said Hattori Hanzō, sitting in an armchair by the fireplace. 'You people seemed more competent in ancient times. What's happened to KillerKnight123's strength, and QueenBee's weapons? Are all of today's Users children who can hardly manage to walk in the snow?'

Arthur wondered briefly why Users, including his sister, always chose virtual names that didn't make sense at all – their names were always a jumble of words, random numbers and aristocratic titles chosen just for the sounds they made. He put the thought aside and tried to answer the mob.

'I have no idea what any previous Users were like, but we're the ones here now,' he said. 'Can you help us or not?'

The man stroked his beard. He seemed very concerned by what Arthur had just said.

'I always feared this day would come,' Hattori said finally. 'The day when there would be so much chaos in every world that Herobrine could try to return. You said he's appeared in your dreams – that leads me to think he's already strong enough for others to feel his presence in the Overworld.'

'That's why we need your help,' said Punk-Princess166. 'We have to defeat the Red King. He might try to bring Herobrine back here.'

Hattori Hanzō laughed. 'You mention the name of the wicked one, but you have no concept of what he's really like,' he said. 'Herobrine thrives on chaos. Everything the Red King has done so far – his monsters and his machines – is paving the way for the arrival of his master. You won't be able to defeat Herobrine. Even the two First Users and an army could only imprison him in the Nether.'

'So,' said Punk-Princess166, 'this is our chance to defeat this guy once and for all. Let us use the sword and fight against the Red King, and ruin Herobrine's chances before he comes out of his stinky cell.'

Arthur hoped that what his sister had said would persuade Hattori; they were running out of time.

Soon it would be nightfall, and Amelia was waiting for them on the other side of the hill.

The old man lifted his sword and slid his hand slowly over its blade, deep in thought, as though pondering over what he had just heard. 'The Red King is a User like you, and he has already searched for the Diamond Sword. So why should I trust you?'

There's no reason why you should trust us, thought Arthur. *We're just two strangers coming out of nowhere and asking for the sword you've kept hidden for years, without any proof we're not going to use it to commit a crime or destroy the world.* Perhaps they should give up on trying to persuade Hattori and look for another option.

'What can we say?' Arthur said eventually. 'That we're evil psychopaths with delusions of grandeur? If we really were, we wouldn't tell you that. It's your choice: you can either trust us or wait for Herobrine and the Red King to achieve everything they've always wanted.'

Hattori Hanzō rose, walking towards the fireplace and placing his sword on a wooden frame. He stood there for a moment, with his back turned to Arthur and Punk-Princess166 as they waited eagerly for an answer.

'I, Hattori Hanzō, the last guardian, will help you in this battle,' he said. His voice was calm but firm. 'I swore that my own sword would protect Users, and once again I am called upon to honour that pledge. However, we have one problem. I hid the Diamond Sword in a secret place on a hill, about two days' walk from here.'

And, for the first time since they arrived in the ice biome, Arthur grinned. 'I know just the person to help with that problem,' he said, shaking Hattori's hand. 'For a fair price, that is – including interest.'

CHAPTER 24

ARROWS ON THE ICE

Hattori Hanzō agreed to walk with Arthur and Punk-Princess166 to Amelia's balloon and fly to the place where he'd hidden Herobrine's sword. Then they would have to travel for two days until they reached City 01. Once there, they would fight against the Red King and bring peace back to the Overworld.

When you put it like that, Arthur thought to himself, *it doesn't seem so hard*. But there were lots of details that could go wrong.

'Are you ready?' asked Hattori. 'There's only an hour of sunlight left – just enough for us to get to your friend's hot-air balloon before the monsters come out.'

Arthur and Punk-Princess166 nodded, though they were reluctant to leave the cabin's warmth and head back out into the cold. Thankfully, the mob had given them scarves and some old gloves, so it would be much better than their journey there. Hattori Hanzō followed them out, dressed all in black and carrying his sword on his back. He wore the expression of a man ready for battle.

'I didn't know you were a ninja,' said Punk-Princess166. 'That style suits you.'

'Don't be silly, girl,' Hattori replied. 'Ninjas have no honour. I'm a samurai, the last guardian of the ancient paths of the Overworld.'

'Oh. Your clothes look like ninja clothes,' said Punk-Princess166.

'Well . . .' The mob cleared his throat. 'There is a possibility that those dishonourable ninjas and I buy our clothes from the same tailor. He's the cheapest.'

Arthur laughed, trying to picture the sort of shop that ninjas and samurai would go to for their clothes. He shook away the thought and carried on walking beside Hattori and his sister. He thought about how much had changed since they'd arrived in the Overworld, all the new things he had done and all the people he'd met whose daily lives were so different from his own – and from everybody else's in the real world. It struck him that, in this strange pixelated world that made no sense, he'd discovered an unknown part of himself – a part that spoke of adventure and swordsmen, and that fought against evil kings and ancient demons.

'We're nearly there,' said Hattori. 'The hill is just over there.'

They trudged up the slope where the old man had knocked them down earlier, slipping on the stones. The samurai just hopped from one stone to the next, reaching the top in an instant, as if the obstacles were minor irritations and hardly a challenge at all.

'I'd love to be able to do that,' said Arthur. 'I'd never be late for school again.'

'Amen,' his sister replied.

Sliding and tripping, it took them about ten minutes to reach the top. The sun was setting, and the last thing they needed was for monsters to appear through the snow. Arthur dreaded the idea of a creeper, zombie, enderman or spider showing up right then. They upped their pace, running on the ice as fast as they could, only stopping when Arthur or his sister fell down. Thankfully, Amelia's balloon was in sight and not too far away now. The only problem was . . . she seemed ready to take off.

'Hey, wait for us!' shouted Arthur. 'Wait for us!'

The balloon had already risen a little above the ground; the sunlight was almost gone. They ran as fast as they could, waving their arms in the air and hoping Amelia could see them. If they didn't reach Amelia soon, she'd leave and would only come back to get them the following morning – forcing them to spend the night there.

'We'd better run,' said Punk-Princess166. '*Fast!*'

'I know, I know!' Arthur shouted.

They were less than ten metres away from the balloon now, so they could see Amelia clearly as she removed the sandbags she'd used as anchors. The inflated balloon was ready to take off. Arthur was about to call out for help again when suddenly all his attention shifted at the sound of a scream beside him. His sister's voice tore through the air; it was so piercing that it made both Arthur and Hattori Hanzō stop in their tracks instantly. Punk-Princess166 was kneeling on the ice with something stuck in her left shoulder. It was an arrow!

Arthur ran towards her as fast as he could and helped her up. 'I need you to carry on walking, Mallu,' he said, holding her round the waist. 'It's just a little bit further until we get to the balloon.'

'I know, you idiot,' she replied. 'And my name is Punk-Princess166.'

'Maybe save being annoying for when you haven't got an arrow in your shoulder,' Arthur told her.

He looked around and saw shapes looming suddenly out of the darkness. He didn't stop to count them, but there were lots of them, and they were everywhere – approaching fast. They were skeletons, with bows and arrows aimed at the three of them. He could hear the sound of bowstrings being pulled back and the whistle of arrows slicing through the air, each one flying closer to the Users.

'Run, you fools!' shouted Hattori Hanzō. 'I will

deal with these worms. It's about time I gave the Dazzling Flight of Ender the Dragon a try.'

Arthur looked back and saw the samurai standing ready for battle, sword in hand, as several skeletons closed in on him. He hoped the old man had the skill it would take to escape unscathed; but, as he tried to reach the balloon just a few metres away, his main concern was getting his sister to safety.

'It's night-time already,' said Amelia when they arrived. 'You're late. Why didn't you stay at the old man's house until morning?'

She stopped talking when she saw the wound on Punk-Princess166's shoulder. She pushed down the edge of the basket to help Arthur get his sister inside, making sure the arrow didn't go any deeper. 'What's going on?' she asked them. 'Where's the sword?'

'It's a long story, Amelia,' Arthur replied. 'But right now I need you to wait here a bit longer. We've got a guest.'

There was no time for explanations. Suddenly the wind surged, and snow and ice were flung everywhere in a blinding blast. Arthur covered his face with his hand, waiting for the next crashing wave, but there was silence. Not even the sound of skeletons or arrows – just the wind.

'Hello?' shouted Arthur.

At first there was no response. Then suddenly something loomed against the ice – a figure dressed in black with a sword in his hand.

The samurai was on his way, leaving behind him a heap of dead skeletons torn to pieces by the flawless blows of the master swordsman. He drew a handkerchief from his pocket and wiped the blade clean before getting into the balloon. He didn't have a single scratch on his face or a speck of dirt on his clothes.

'The Dazzling Flight of Ender the Dragon,' he said. 'The best offensive strike my master ever taught me – powerful enough to beat twenty enemies at once.' He turned to Amelia. 'Madam, it's a pleasure to see you again.'

'The pleasure's all mine, old warrior,' the mercenary replied.

Amelia headed to the controls and the balloon began to ascend fast, rising higher and higher like a dandelion seed blown by a strong wind. The white world beneath them was left behind, just as all its monsters began to emerge.

'I hate to interrupt your reunion,' said Punk-Princess166, 'but I've got an arrow in my shoulder. And it hurts.'

Amelia and Hattori Hanzō pushed Arthur aside and began treating his sister's wound, combining the samurai's expertise with cuts and bruises with the mercenary's first-aid skills. Within minutes Punk-Princess166 had makeshift stitches, and the blood had stopped gushing from her shoulder. She was still in a lot of pain, but the worst was over – the wound wouldn't kill her.

Everything was OK.

Or so they thought.

CONCEPTS OF THE OVERWORLD

PART EIGHT: Skeletons

By Punk-Princess166

Skeletons are horrible things. At least creepers look you in the face as they try to kill you – they have a little honour left as they pursue their victims. But skeletons are different: they keep away from you and try to hit you with their arrows from afar.

Once you manage to get close to them with a good sword, it's relatively easy to destroy them, but the problem is getting close enough in the first place – before you get there, you may be hit several times. My best tip for dealing with skeletons is to wait until daylight takes care of them – however, if this fails, do what you can to dodge the arrows, and knock those idiots down.

CHAPTER 25

SMOOTH LANDING

For a while everything seemed to be going all right. Punk-Princess166's wound had been well treated and their journey through that white vastness wasn't as tricky as Arthur had assumed it would be – no skeletons, no wicked tyrants and no lords from the Nether. They just continued on their way. Arthur sat beside his sister as she slept, gazing out at the nocturnal world and the great ice structures beneath them: high mountains and deep valleys, everything made of white on white. Amelia and Hattori Hanzō talked about the route, adjusting the controls as they searched for the base that the samurai had built to hold the sword and other memories from the first war against Herobrine.

Arthur rose and walked over to the samurai and the pilot. He was still worried about what they would do once they found the sword. Neither he nor his sister knew anything about battles, sword fighting or any kind of combat. They were just two kids who had spent most of their lives in their flat or at school.

'Hattori,' he said, 'I don't think we can defeat Herobrine or the Red King, not even with the sword. Did you see what happened back there? If it hadn't been for you, my sister and I would be dead now.'

The mob sat with his legs crossed and his hands on his knees. He looked at the sky, and then back down at Arthur.

'Winning or losing doesn't fall to a weapon,' said the samurai. 'Any young person with a heart and a mind in the right place can defeat an army. I've met Users before you and your sister who were skilled warriors and knew a lot about the Overworld. But what enabled them to defeat Herobrine was the fact that they were ready to fight until the end without wavering. That's where the true strength of a warrior lies. I couldn't have defeated a single skeleton if I had already made up my mind not to win.'

Arthur shook his head; he didn't believe that it really worked that way. 'I'm not like them,' he replied. 'I'm not like you either. Being scared is all I've done since I got here.'

'You've done a lot more than be scared. I saw you stand up for yourself, and as far as I know, you've already survived several challenges before finding me. You're not seeing the whole picture.' Hattori Hanzō stretched out his legs and stroked his beard. 'There are many people in your world, I believe. Some are older than you and your sister, some younger, some stronger and some weaker. But it was you two who were called to the Overworld – that's a chance not many people are given. What you do with this opportunity is what defines you. A certain User turned into the Red King, but I hope you can do better than that.'

Arthur nodded and gazed at the lightening sky; dawn was one of his favourite moments in the Overworld. He loved to stare at the sun as its strange shape rose in the sky. He'd been in this universe so long that at times he had to remind himself things were different in the real world – the sun wasn't square and monsters didn't come out after nightfall. He worried that one day he'd wake up and feel he belonged here, that the Overworld was his home; what if he lost the feeling of emptiness in his chest that drove him to find a way back to the real world?

'We're nearly there,' Hattori announced. 'Look – that's the fortress I built.'

Arthur woke his sister up and pointed to their destination. 'We're nearly home,' he told her. 'We'll just get the sword and then we'll be there.'

Punk-Princess166 turned her sleepy half-closed eyes towards her brother. She yawned. 'Is that what you woke me up for?' she asked. 'Let me sleep for another five minutes, pleeease . . .'

Arthur let her go back to sleep and stared at Hattori Hanzō's fortress. It was a giant box made of stones several metres tall. On the roof was a design of two crossed swords, a white one and a blue one. It was much larger than the cabin where the samurai lived. There were more torches around it too – they generated enough light to frighten off any monster that might ever emerge around there.

'Crew, get ready for landing,' said Amelia. 'We're already descending, so hold on tight.'

The balloon was losing height. Amelia took note of the winds here and there, fixing the route using the two thousand keys and levers on the control panel. The descent was so precise and smooth that Arthur hardly even felt his usual fear of flying. In fact, he had even started to enjoy travelling this way – perhaps it was because it meant they were far from the ground where monsters might appear out of the blue.

About ten minutes later they touched down, landing smoothly on the ice fewer than twenty metres away from the fortress. Two sturdy iron gates kept intruders away. After all the sandbags had been placed on the floor to anchor the balloon, everyone got out, eager to see the sword that had caused everyone so many problems.

'I hope this sword is worth all this trouble,' said Punk-Princess166. 'I hope it sings and makes coffee or something. A cup of coffee is exactly what I need right now.'

The four of them strode quickly to Hattori's base, too excited to feel the cold. Arthur thought back through everything that had happened on their way to this spot, all the people who had helped them – Alex the priestess and Steve the warrior, who had given up his life to save Arthur from the horde of zombies. He thanked them all silently as he walked.

'Hold on,' said Hattori Hanzō. 'From here onward, there are spells cast by a witch to protect the base.'

'Are they deadly?' asked Amelia, sounding curious.

'They're just here to frighten off strangers,' the samurai said. He made a snowball and hurled it at the fortress, but before it reached the stone wall there was a massive blast and the snowball vanished.

'Does that answer your question?' Hattori asked.

'Yes, sir,' the pilot replied. 'It certainly does.'

Hattori drew his sword and walked to the invisible wall, then touched it with the point of his weapon. 'In the name of the two Users and Hattori

Hanzō, guardian of Herobrine's sword . . . In the name of the blood that has come before and shall come after me . . . Open!'

Arthur wondered whether the cold had sent the man crazy, given that he'd started talking to walls that blew up, but to his surprise a reddish glow appeared around the building and its iron gates opened. They all stood there for over a minute, waiting for something to come out and kill them. But nothing did, so they headed towards the entrance to the fortress.

'I can't believe we've come this far,' said Punk-Princess166. 'This should be our return ticket to a decent bath and junk food.'

They walked into the base with eyes only for one thing. Inside the fortress was a massive space filled with all kinds of objects – dusty suits of armour, all types of swords, pictures and even some precious stones that Arthur saw Amelia slipping into her pocket . . . not that Arthur cared about Amelia's dishonesty just then. They searched for the sword in every nook and cranny.

'I can't find this sword anywhere,' said Punk-

Princess166. 'Are you sure there isn't some other fortress around here?'

'It had to be well hidden in case someone managed to enter my base, even with all my safety measures.'

'Guess that makes sense, grandpa,' Punk Princess166 said.

The samurai placed his hand on a wooden table and smiled. He pushed the table aside and began hitting the floor with his sword until the block beneath turned to dust.

'The sword is exactly where I left it,' he said. 'After so many decades and so many battles, my job as a guardian ends here.'

Arthur and the others watched as Hattori's hand disappeared into the hole and then emerged holding something. It was bigger and more beautiful than any of them had imagined – a work of art in its own right, and yet it could still destroy armies. After all they had gone through, there – before their eyes at last – lay Herobrine's sword.

CHAPTER 26

THE SWORD OF HEROBRINE

Arthur stared at the sword for a long time, hypnotized. It was large and rectangular with a diamond blade and a golden hilt engraved with countless details and indecipherable symbols. Hattori Hanzō held it with care, as if it might explode at any moment.

'Forged of iron from the Nether and soaked in the dragon's blood,' said the samurai. 'Here is the sword that banished Herobrine from the Overworld.'

The mob let Arthur hold the sword for a moment. Despite its size it was as light as a feather. He could feel something like a power surge going through the sword, as if it knew it was in the hands of a User and was curious to find out who now held it after so long locked in the dark.

'Don't fall in love with the sword, kid,' said Amelia. 'If you fall in love in the snow it won't last – I learned that the hard way.'

'I'm not,' he lied. 'It's just a sword. What's there to fall in love with about an old sword more ancient than my grandpa?'

'If you say so, kid,' Amelia replied.

Then it was Punk-Princess166's turn. She took full advantage of the opportunity and posed with the sword as if she was fighting against invisible enemies, but not for long – her shoulder was still very painful, so she gave the weapon back to the samurai. After checking that everything was as they had found it, the troupe got ready to leave.

'I never thought we'd make it,' said Arthur. 'All we need to do now is get to City 01 and use the Red King's portal.'

'And defeat the Red King,' added his sister.

'Sure. Easy.'

They left the fortress, buzzing with excitement. Hattori Hanzō even began whistling a song, as if for the first time he could afford to walk with the world's weight off his shoulders. But their good moods faded as soon as they stepped out and looked towards the hot-air balloon. Or, rather, what was left of it.

The balloon was shredded into withered pieces on the ground. Beside it, dragging itself over the snow with its arms swinging, was an enderman – the same one that had destroyed Steve's village. It stood still and turned its malevolent gaze on the group of adventurers.

They didn't move; they didn't know what to do in the face of the enderman's return.

'It destroyed my . . .' Amelia trailed off. She couldn't believe her eyes. 'All right,' she said, 'I think it's time for someone to die.'

The enderman materialized just a step away from them, using that teleporting skill which always stunned the Users. The enderman was so close to Arthur that he could see every detail of every pixel on its body, every little square and right angle that made up the most terrifying creature in the Red King's army.

'Hello, Users. What a pleasure to speak to you again at the end of this journey.' The enderman's mouth moved, but the voice that came through it was the Red King's. The voice was calm; he lingered over every syllable, stretching out the words as though he was relishing them. The monster stared at each of the adventurers, moving its gaze from Hattori Hanzō to Punk-Princess166, as if trying to figure them out.

'We're too busy for this right now, moron,' said Arthur's sister. 'Maybe call later.'

The enderman burst out laughing. Hearing that sound coming from an expressionless, soulless creature was terrifying. Arthur wondered if the monster felt anything at all – if something inside it wanted to rebel against its ruler.

'You make me laugh,' came the answer. 'I always knew you wanted to use the sword against me rather than hand it over. I know all about your plan – a pathetic plan, by the way. My enderman has followed you silently since you left the village – he is my eyes and ears. All I needed was for you to lead me to the sword. Give it to me and I'll let you go.'

Arthur shook his head. He wasn't going to let the Red King take the sword after all they had gone through to get it. He would never let Herobrine be freed from the Nether.

'I think you'd better get lost,' he answered. 'We've got a samurai, a mercenary and . . . my sister. Four against one.'

The enderman laughed again; the awful sound was so deafening that it shook the ground. The creature returned to stillness and faced Arthur. 'I hope you enjoy eternity in the Nether,' it said. 'I will slay you all, and use the sword to bring Herobrine back to the Overworld.'

Before Arthur could react, the creature had disappeared, like lightning piercing through the sky. Arthur knew they could be attacked from any direction, so he drew the sword and held it with both hands, watching for any movement on the edges of his vision.

'Stay together,' shouted Hattori Hanzō. 'That damned creature wants to catch us unawares!'

The enderman appeared suddenly in front of the samurai and tried to strike a blow, but the old man was faster – he dodged and stabbed at the enderman's face with his sword. But, even though the blow was a good one, it hardly helped them. The blade touched the enderman's skin but nothing happened, and once again the creature disappeared.

'Be on guard,' shouted Amelia. 'He's trying to find out who is the weakest, like an animal chasing a herd.'

Arthur looked around and saw the mercenary draw a knife from her jacket pocket. He couldn't see how that was going to help them fight against something so enormous. Punk-Princess166 stood to his left, trying to hold a sword in one hand and fighting to cope with the pain in her shoulder. She didn't seem afraid, but then, she was never afraid of anything. It had always been this way: Mallu being fearless while Arthur was terrified. And that was exactly how he felt now, his sweaty hands shivering.

'Arthur!'

His sister snapped him back to reality, but it was too late. The enderman was right in front of him, an inescapable shadow, his square hand stretching out to grab Arthur's neck.

One thought kept playing over and over in Arthur's head, beating like a drum, hammered relentlessly into his brain. Just three words: *I will die*. He gathered his strength, remembering that he held in his hands the most powerful weapon of all time. The sword made him change that thought to – *I don't want to die*.

He allowed that phrase to take over instead, repeating it again and again. Then he shut his eyes and lifted Herobrine's sword, wielding it against the enderman, and he felt its blade pierce through tough, hard layers of pixel . . .

Arthur took a deep breath.

He hoped from the bottom of his heart that he had done enough. Cautiously, one at a time, he opened his eyes, shaking from head to toe. The enderman was still standing, but things were different now. The creature put its hand on its stomach, right on the spot where the sword had done its job. Terrifying screams poured from the monster's mouth as it staggered; it couldn't do anything except groan in pain. Then, with a mighty thud, the monster finally fell to the ground, dead.

'OK, I didn't expect that,' said Punk-Princess166. 'I want a sword just like that one, please.'

Arthur stared at the dark body in the snow. The purple eyes no longer shone; the monster was motionless. They had won the battle. It had only taken one blow to knock down the most dangerous monster from the Red King's army. But there was still one question that they needed to confront: how on earth were they going to leave the ice biome now the enderman had shredded Amelia's hot-air balloon?

CHAPTER 27

THE HEART WILL TAKE US FAR

Hattori Hanzō was the first person to congratulate Arthur. The old man patted him on the shoulder and smiled, which was pretty rare for Hattori. They all gathered around Arthur then, staring at the sword in fascination. They had never seen an enderman defeated so easily before.

'Imagine what the Red King would do if he got hold of this sword,' said Amelia. 'Ruling over the Overworld would be as easy as burning down a thatched cottage. I think we'd better grab that thing and run far away, where he can never find us.'

'We have to fight,' said Punk-Princess166. 'This is the best chance we have – it's now or never.'

'I agree with the girl,' answered Hattori Hanzō.

Arthur had already thought of what Amelia had suggested. Even then he was tempted by the idea, but he didn't want to spend the rest of his life locked in this world, living like a fugitive. They had a weapon that could finish off the Red King once and for all – they just needed to get close enough. Which was going to be hard now the balloon had been completely destroyed.

'We're going to fight,' Arthur said. 'We have the sword – we can't waste this opportunity. But we have a problem. How can we get to City 01 and defeat the Red King if the balloon's trashed and we're stuck in the middle of the ice?'

The others looked at one another. None of them had really thought about that problem yet – they'd been distracted by the power of the sword and the possibilities it opened up. But those possibilities would never be fulfilled unless they could find a way off the ice. Arthur wondered whether there was anything in Hattori Hanzō's base that might be useful, but he only remembered seeing some works of art, weapons and other objects that would be no use to them right now.

'We can walk,' said the samurai. 'I've done the journey from here to the next biome before – it takes just over three weeks on foot. It isn't difficult. We can eat bears and wolves on the way, battling against nature, as we always are.'

Amelia was the first to respond. She didn't seem particularly happy with the old man's idea – her expression was a mixture of anger and disbelief. 'Or we can try to mend the balloon,' she said. 'It won't be perfect, but it's better than walking around – we'd be killed on the first night.'

Arthur didn't know what to make of it all. Neither option was good enough – both would give the Red King plenty of time to rearm and prepare his defence. No, they had to get to him before he was ready to fight against Herobrine's sword. Arthur stood in silence, thinking things over and imagining all the options that they didn't have.

'I've got an idea,' said Punk-Princess166. 'And if it works, you're going to have to call me a genius for the rest of your lives.'

All eyes turned to her. None of them really believed that there could be a practical solution to the problem. Punk-Princess166 walked towards Arthur and took the sword without saying a word, handling it carefully to make sure her shoulder wound didn't get worse. With firm steps, she strode to the enderman's body, dragging the sword point along the ground as she went.

'When I used to play Minecraft on the computer, every time I managed to kill an enderman something happened,' she said. 'They used to leave a pearl behind – a pearl that could take you anywhere you liked.'

'What?' asked Arthur. 'How can that be possible?'

'You should've been playing the game yourself instead of bothering me every time I was playing,' his sister replied. 'It would've made you much more useful right now.'

She thrust the sword into the dead enderman's chest. It was hard to cut right down to its stomach, so Amelia and the samurai helped her. The smell of rotten flesh rose, and Arthur fought the urge to vomit. It was the worst smell he had ever come across. But it didn't end there: Punk-Princess166 bent over and slid her hand into the wound, groping for something inside. When she withdrew her arm, it was covered up to the elbow in black goo.

'That is the most disgusting thing I have ever seen,' Arthur said.

'I have to agree with you on that, kid,' Amelia replied.

After searching inside the creature's body for a minute or so, Punk-Princess166 pulled out a huge pearl. She lifted it with a triumphant expression and a smile that might well have led a psychologist to question her sanity. The rest of them gathered around her, staring at the glowing pearl soaked in the enderman's black blood.

'I knew it would be there,' Punk-Princess166 said. 'Our ticket to City 01, where we can kick the king's butt.'

'How does it work?' Hattori Hanzō asked. 'How is it possible that I have lived in the Overworld for so long and never heard of it?'

'Don't worry, grandpa, my uncles are younger than you but they don't even know how to use the internet,' Punk-Princess166 said as she turned to explain it to them all. 'It's dead easy: we all have to touch the pearl and think hard about where we would like to go. In this case, we think about City 01. Just think about the city and the pearl will take us there. Do not think about the Red King – he will be heavily guarded and so we want to catch him unawares.'

Arthur agreed with his sister – it seemed like the best plan was to sneak into the city and find out as much as they could before attacking. Turning up in a room guarded by endermen, creepers and other monsters didn't sound great. They had to be smart.

'I like that idea,' said Amelia. 'Sounds like my best chance of being reimbursed for the damage done to my balloon.'

'I think it's a good idea too,' said Hattori Hanzō. 'I'm ready to wield my sword against the enemy who plans to destroy my world.'

Arthur nodded and joined his sister, the samurai and the mercenary. Punk-Princess166 stretched her arm out, holding the pearl, and asked everyone to touch its surface, thinking hard about their final destination. They stepped forward, mobs and humans working together to save the Overworld from destruction. Each of them did what had been asked, concentrating on where they wanted to go.

They heard a noise like the sound of a laser beam from a Hollywood movie, or a *Star Wars* lightsaber. Then Arthur felt like he was bending upward, as though he was taking off in a plane without a seatbelt. Every part of his body was shaking and burning. It was the exact same feeling he'd experienced as he was drawn into the Overworld.

He tried to focus all his thoughts on City 01 and how much he wanted to get there. He repeated the name of the city over and over again like a mantra; there was no room for error.

The journey came to an end as quickly as it had begun. In under a second they had arrived.

They were in the throne room, right under the Red King's nose.

CHAPTER 28

THE SWORD AND THE KING

At first no one moved. They just stared at the figure before them. He was a User like Arthur and his sister, dressed in red clothes with a golden crown on his head. His hair was gold and his eyes were deep blue. He looked older than Arthur, perhaps sixteen or seventeen years old. Sitting on his throne of black blocks with a ruby sword on his lap, he smiled down at the group.

'You've saved me a lot of work,' said the Red King. 'It would have taken my army a long time to find you.'

At the sound of the king's voice Arthur clenched his fists. He couldn't believe that this boy was behind everything – a boy not even much older than him, just a human User who knew nothing about anything.

Punk-Princess166 ignored the enemy and turned to her friends. 'How did we end up here?' she asked. 'I told you very clearly not to think about this guy.'

Hattori Hanzō shrugged his shoulders. 'It's hard not to think about something when someone specifically tells you not to.'

'I thought samurai were masters of self-control,' Punk-Princess166 said.

Arthur ignored the blame game and looked around. The throne hall was enormous; it was made of red blocks and decorated with hundreds of precious stones, suits of armour and extravagant chandeliers. It was also packed with servants – endermen stood in each corner watching the invaders with hostile eyes. But what really caught Arthur's eye was a black stone arch in the centre of the room. It was bare, without any detail on its surface.

'Hand the sword to me and you won't be killed,' said the Red King. 'As a sign of my goodwill, I will open the portal so that you can get back home.'

'What if we wanted to get rid of your army and then use a portal?' said Punk-Princess166. 'We have Herobrine's sword. You don't.'

'And you owe me a balloon!' shouted Amelia.

The Red King rose and pointed to the arch; the endermen followed every move he made.

'That's the only portal left,' he said. 'I made sure all the others were destroyed. If there's a way for you to get back home, it's through this portal. You have no choice but to give in and hand me the sword. Then you can get back to your miserable lives and never return to this world, which is no more than data in your computer. Just a game.'

Arthur shook his head and grabbed the sword from his sister's hands. The Overworld wasn't just a game. He couldn't think of it that way, not after what he'd been through with the two mobs beside him, not after meeting Alex . . . and Steve. He couldn't allow the Red King to treat it as just a game.

'I will never hand the sword over to a selfish idiot like you,' he said. 'I'm going to end you, and all your lackeys too. Then we'll get back home on our own terms.'

'What a pity,' replied the Red King. 'Be prepared to taste your death, User – for your sake, I hope it is brief.'

The Red King lifted his sword and walked towards them; four endermen followed him, appearing and disappearing around their master. There was no way out – they had to fight for their lives and for the Overworld.

'If this is the end,' said Amelia, 'I hope there's a big trunk full of gems on the other side.'

'A warrior is never afraid of the end,' said Hattori Hanzō. 'He fights without fear or reluctance; he becomes the sword.'

'I love that phrase,' said Punk-Princess166. 'Remind me to put it on a fridge magnet.'

Arthur, Punk-Princess166, Amelia and Hattori Hanzō drew their swords, ready for anything.

'Be smart,' said Arthur. 'They won't have mercy on us – we have to fight hard.'

The first blade to strike was Arthur's against the king's; it struck hard and sent sparks into the air. Blow after blow, Herobrine's sword smashed against the king's blade while Punk-Princess166 and the others fought against the endermen as best they could.

'You don't stand a chance,' said the Red King. 'You can hardly use the sword. If you had any other weapon, you would be dead already, you fool.'

He's right, thought Arthur. It was as if the sword knew what it had to do to keep its owner alive, guiding his hand every time he attacked or shielded himself. It was a living sword! All Arthur had to do was trust that the sword would defeat the Red King – he had to trust the weapon that had banished Herobrine.

'Why do you want to destroy the Overworld?' Arthur said.

'I don't want to destroy it, I just want to turn it into an empire to rule for a thousand years. The temporary destruction is merely the price we have to pay for good. I'm saving this place.'

'You're insane.' Arthur wanted to say more but couldn't – he realized the endermen had injured and cornered his friends, and were now preparing to kill them. Arthur turned his head and shouted his sister's name, but he paid a huge price for his distraction.

The Red King took advantage of the opportunity and kicked Arthur's hand, hard. The sword flew away from him. An instant later Arthur took an elbow to the stomach and fell to the ground writhing in pain, giving the enemy the chance to move forward and grab the sword of Herobrine.

The Red King burst out laughing. 'Endermen, hold,' he ordered. 'I'd like these worms to relish my victory and witness the birth of my empire.'

Arthur watched the monsters halt in their attack, disappearing with that whip-crack sound. The Users and their friends were now alone with the king, the golden-haired young man standing in front of the portal. Alone and defeated.

'What are we going to do?' asked Amelia as they all ran towards Arthur. 'We've got to take the sword from him.'

'There's nothing we can do,' Arthur replied. 'We did exactly what he hoped we would do, and we lost. He knew he could beat us even if we had the sword.'

The Red King stood before the large arch, touched it with the sword and murmured the same phrases several times. Arthur had heard some of the words before.

'Dreaming even in death, Herobrine awaits in his castle in the Nether. I call upon you, death who walks. And with the sword that destroyed you, I place you under my rule.'

Punk-Princess166 helped Arthur up. There was a cracking sound, and a purple light glowed inside the arch, shimmering and spinning. The portal was working – its light shone brightly. A figure loomed through from the other side. His limbs began to take shape slowly in the Overworld. First came his arms and legs, then the image of a mob steadily formed as the line blurred between different realities and universes. And that was how, with their hearts pounding, they saw Herobrine take his first step out of the Nether.

CHAPTER 29

HEROBRINE

Herobrine was exactly as he had been in Arthur's dream: a white-eyed, distorted version of Steve. He was wearing a black overcoat with a hood that made his eyes all the more frightening, like two burning suns. They all stared at him; the visitor did not speak, he just stared at each and every face, block after block, as though he were relishing his first minute away from the lava and the fire.

'I think we're in trouble,' said Punk-Princess166. 'I hope you all have life insurance.'

'The Overworld is lost, young lady,' Hattori Hanzō said. 'We can only sit and watch the tide of destruction that is about to begin.'

The Red King walked over to the creature.

'Herobrine,' he said haughtily, 'I have set you free and the sword is mine. I order you to kill these worms. Show me your power.'

Arthur took a deep breath, waiting for his head to be cut off, but nothing happened. On the contrary, the monster was staring at the king, as though it had finally dawned on him that he was there. Herobrine lifted his right arm and threw the Red King clean across the hall. He smashed into the wall on the far side and fell to the ground, unconscious.

Herobrine gestured once and the sword was back in his hand. 'No one can control me, you insect.'

Herobrine's voice was powerful, as though it had been amplified by a sound box; it was metallic and emotionless. The creature turned his attention to the others then, drawing closer to Arthur and his friends. His face was expressionless, but no doubt he was pleased by everything that had happened.

'And so I come across these Users again,' said Herobrine. 'It's a pleasure seeing you in person, Arthur. I hope I live up to your expectations.'

The group stepped back and huddled close

together, as if that could make some kind of difference to their plight.

'I'm sorry, but the pleasure's not reciprocated,' Arthur said. 'You're free now – you don't need to hurt anyone or destroy the world. We can live together in peace.'

Herobrine laughed. 'I'm afraid we can't live together, young User,' he answered. 'I am an ancient being – it would be like a mouse wanting to live with a tiger. No, I am chaos who walks, and I have come to finish what I had started: destroying all universes – the Overworld, and your world too. Everything will fall.'

Punk-Princess166 stepped forward and faced the enemy, trying to hide her fear. 'We won't let you do that, you square-head,' she said. 'You've been defeated once, and believe me, lightning can strike the same place twice.'

Arthur pulled his sister's hand; maybe they should be trying to escape and find a new way of fighting. They had been defeated by the Red King, they had lost the sword – there was nothing they could do. They had to get back to Alex and seek help. He thought about trying to come up with a new strategy, but really it all boiled down to whether they would make it out of the hall alive.

'Cheeky girl,' said Herobrine. 'I'd like to see what chance you stand against me, you –'

Herobrine didn't get the chance to finish. Moving so stealthily that nobody noticed him, the Red King had crept back across the hall and thrust a sword into Herobrine's back. Smiling, he pushed the blade deeper.

'I brought you back to this world, worm,' he said. 'All you had to do was obey me – but now I'll have to kill you.'

'You foolish human, do you think you can beat me with that?' Herobrine said.

This was exactly the moment Arthur was waiting for – they could let Herobrine and the Red King kill each other while they ran away! Arthur took one look at the king and Herobrine fighting viciously, then signalled to the others. They broke into a run towards the grand double door. They had to escape from the hall – they could come up with another plan once they'd got out.

'We can't fight against the two of them now,' he told the others. 'Let's go and hide at Alex's and then we can think about what to do next.'

'You're right, boy,' replied Hattori Hanzō. 'There is a time to fight and a time to withdraw. This is just the first battle of the war – there will be other opportunities to fight against our enemy.'

'So we're going to run like crazy,' said Amelia. 'Sounds like a good plan to me.'

The fierce battle continued on the other side of the hall, furniture and decorations being destroyed, swords clashing together over and over as each side refused to surrender. The four endermen had come back to help their master, making a powerful attack. Arthur and Punk-Princess166 were already opening the hall doors when they heard Herobrine's voice.

'Before we part, Users, I'd like to give you a gift. Something small to remember me by.'

Herobrine stared at the humans, his eyes glowing intensely, until a flash of light blasted through the room. Arthur shut his eyes as he pushed open the door . . . and found himself in a large room packed with zombies. He could tell what they were by the sounds they made, those horrible grunts that reminded him of the mine where Steve had lost his life.

'Amelia,' said Hattori Hanzō. 'Lead the Users. I will see to these disgusting creatures.'

Arthur felt the mercenary take his hand, and he knew she was holding his sister's too. He could hear the zombies approaching as the samurai drew his sword. He let Amelia lead them away to the sounds of Hattori's sword knocking zombies down. The walking dead didn't stand a chance. By the time Arthur looked back, the enemies were lying on the floor and the samurai was wiping his sword clean on his shirt.

They went through endless halls, trying to avoid being spotted by the guards, and Hattori fought against zombies and skeletons whenever they came across them. As they went, they could still hear the battle between their two enemies, and they hoped it would keep going for a while longer yet.

'We're nearly there,' said Amelia. 'I think this is the first time I've ever been on the king's side. I hope he finishes off that creep with the glowing eyes.'

Punk-Princess166 laughed. 'I hope they both kill each other,' she said.

A few minutes later they reached a road, and City 01 lay before them for the first time. It was horrible and ugly. There were broken machines everywhere, and everything was made of rusty iron. Giant screens carrying the image of the Red King were spaced along the roads, and the whole place was littered with rubbish. The sky was dark; clouds of pollution gases drifted through the air; you could see rats running around freely on the streets and all the mobs looked dejected and exhausted. So this was the outcome of all the mods that the Red King wanted to spread across the world.

'A house mirrors the soul of its inhabitant, my master used to say,' Hattori Hanzō said. 'And now I can see that he was right.'

Arthur thought about saying something clever, but ended up saying nothing at all. He began to drift off, his eyelids closing, everything fading, as though he was falling, falling, falling . . .

The last thing he saw was something flying over them – something with glowing eyes that burned like two suns . . .

EPILOGUE

WHAT ARE WE?

Arthur woke up feeling great. His body didn't hurt at all; everything seemed to have healed, probably thanks to some remedy Amelia and Hattori must have given him. He was ready to come up with a plan of attack – he would do whatever it took, fighting together with his friends to free the Overworld from the Red King and Herobrine.

'I'm glad you're up, melon head,' he heard his sister say. 'I was getting worried.'

He opened his eyes slowly, expecting to see all the colours and pixels of the Overworld and all the funny square-shaped things that made up that universe. But that wasn't what he saw. His eyes roved about, from his sister to everything else around him, taking in every line and every detail that made up the flat where he had lived all his life. He must be dreaming of home . . . but everything seemed so real.

'I know,' his sister said. 'I was scared when I woke up too. I guess this was Herobrine's gift: sending us back home.'

Arthur sat up straight away. Anger surged through his body. He couldn't leave his friends behind, especially as the Red King was still alive and Herobrine was free. When all of this had started, his dream had been to get back home, back to this very room – but things had changed.

How has this happened? Arthur asked himself. *Why has Herobrine done this?*

Mallu sat down next to him. She looked tired; she wasn't even up to joking around. She stared at the computer on the other side of the living room, as if hoping something would happen, that the lights would begin flashing again and the numbers would reappear.

She sighed. 'He knew he had to get us Users out of there.' Then she paused. 'And so here we are, at home, while Herobrine and the Red King are free to destroy the Overworld however they choose to.'

Arthur walked over to the computer and plugged it in, pressing every key to try and get it to work. 'We have to get back there and find Alex, Amelia and Hattori,' he said. 'We can't let Herobrine win.'

'I've already tried, Arthur,' his sister replied. 'I've already done everything you're doing now – even the floppy disc has disappeared. When I woke up, only five minutes had passed here. It's been two hours since then, which means that the Overworld we knew probably doesn't exist there any longer.'

Arthur froze in shock. He didn't have a clue how many months or years had already passed on the other side since they had left. Herobrine could have already conquered everything while they were here in this empty flat.

'What are we going to do, Mallu?' His voice shook. 'How are we going to help our friends?'

His sister put her hand on his shoulder. She seemed calmer and more composed than Arthur would have expected.

'Well,' she said. 'We can't save the world on an empty stomach. I promise we'll get back to the Overworld and help our friends somehow. But there's only so much we can do right now. So, warrior – let's prepare for when the opportunity comes.'

Arthur stood there, thinking about how much had changed, and how much he missed a world that he hadn't even known existed.

Then he took a deep breath and walked towards the kitchen with his sister. All he could think about were all those he had left behind – Alex, Hattori, Amelia . . . and Steve. He would never forget Steve, the first friend they had made and the first they had lost.

Just then the front door opened and their parents appeared, smiling and carrying shopping bags.

'Hi, folks,' their mother said. 'I bought a few things on the way home. I hope someone is in the mood for chocolate!'

'I'm always in that mood, Mum,' replied Mallu. 'And believe me, chocolate is exactly what I need right now.'

'I hope you two didn't argue,' their dad said. 'It's about time you learned to get along.'

Mallu nudged her brother with her elbow. 'We were too busy trying to save the Overworld from an evil king and a creature from the Nether,' she answered. 'There was a mercenary and a samurai as well, but they were cool.'

'Right, Maria Luísa,' her dad said. 'I'll pretend I understood half of what you just said.'

Arthur saw their mum smile as she headed towards the kitchen with her husband. Now he was sure that they really were back home. Everything was normal again, but every word and every thought was tinged with sadness.

'We're home, Noobie.'

'Yeah, we're home,' Arthur said.

The two of them walked into the kitchen with their heads down, not knowing what to say to one another. But their expressions would have changed completely if they had looked back just for a second, following a flicker in the corners of their eyes.

If they had done that, in that precise moment, they would have seen the computer screen flashing with a peculiar green glow, which was especially odd given that the cables were unplugged again. And, through that glow, they would have seen numbers.

Zeros and ones.

Numbers with a message especially for them.

COMING SOON

Herobrine is getting closer to achieving
his aim: total chaos across the Overworld.
Meanwhile, there are rumours about a
terrifying dragon capable of destroying
the digital world – and perhaps even
the real world too . . .

Can a pair of young Minecraft
fans save us all from Herobrine?
Or will he succeed in destroying the
whole Minecraft world – and our own?

Your story starts here . . .

Do you **love books** and
discovering new stories?
Then **www.puffin.co.uk**
is the place for you . . .

- Thrilling adventures, fantastic fiction
and laugh-out-loud fun

- Brilliant videos featuring your favourite authors
and characters

- Exciting competitions, news, activities,
the Puffin blog and SO MUCH more . . .

 **Listen**

Do you love listening to stories?

Want to know what happens behind the scenes in a recording studio?

Hear funny sound effects, exclusive author interviews and the best books read by famous authors and actors on the **Puffin Podcast** at **www.puffin.co.uk**

#ListenWithPuffin